"Tales of the Seventies"

All of the stories in this collection were started between the years 1970 and 1975. They are a product of that time. None of them were ever finished or put into a final form until many years later. They were all in "draft" status, when my business career took off, and I no longer had the time or inspiration to write. My career in international trade blossomed, and many years passed by without my thinking about writing or storytelling. So the stories in this book remained as drafts in various stages of neglect awaiting completion.

I retired and left the business world, and my interest in writing was rekindled. As fate or luck would have it, I moved and was forced to throw out old "junk" I had kept in storage for years. In the process, I came across a box containing these story drafts written during my youth and read some of them.

Some were familiar and came back into focus immediately. For others I felt as if I was reading them for the first time. Most of them felt fresh and "new" to me even though they were all written more than forty years ago. Finding them inspired me to write again. I sharpened and reworked the drafts to make them more readable. The end result is this little book. They are from a different era. An era without gadgets. An era without technology. An era without a screen in our hands opening windows to the world.

I recently had the book read and reviewed by a wide audience. Delightfully, many different stories were praised and singled out by those who participated in the process. The one most highly enjoyed was **The Cat Burglars**, which is a comic story about two thieves and their adventures stealing a large Ocelot. For me, the title was a toss up between **Tales of the Seventies and the Cat Burglars.**

The stories are all set in California in the 1970's. Some are based on my early life growing up in Southern California and are set in that environment. All of them were written after I moved to San Francisco in 1969, and many are set in the bay area. I imagine with titles like **Blind San Franciscans, and The San Francisco Adventure,** that is obvious. One short story from that pile has become a novel, **The Ghost Town Movie Ranch.** I will be publishing it soon.

The novella, **Yesteryears Snows,** is set in southern Ca. and was begun in 1975. It is very different because it does not have a linear plot. It is not meant to be a story about events, instead it is a story about states of mind. For the protagonist, Jeff, things are disconnected and fuzzy.

This is the objective truth of his life but he is convinced that the opposite is true, and that he alone has clarity of vision. My intent in writing this story was to examine and reveal the workings of a schizophrenic mind engulfed in increasingly heavy drug use. The hero is ill, and those around him, his lover and friends, are oblivious to his problem. They pander to his whims, enabling him to do as he pleases, until he becomes more and more delusional.

Many people in the late 1960's and early 1970's believed that psychotropic drugs were the key to spirituality. This was expressed in a movement begun by Timothy Leary that was later fueled by Carlos Castaneda and countless others. This idea was widely spread to the public in the lyrics of countless songs, and many people bought into the idea that the way to enlightenment could be found by turning on, tuning in and dropping out.

Jeff, the main character of this story, is modelled after a close friend of mine from this time. He believed that the use of LSD and other mind bending drugs held the magic key to understanding the nature of the universe. LSD was a magic pill, and if you took it, all would be revealed. This simple act of ingesting a chemical would bring you enlightenment. One night, I was with "Jeff" and he had taken a large dose of LSD. He emerged from his bedroom holding a book I had lent him. On the back cover of the

book in large bold letters, was the word **"ESCAPE"**. He
pointed the book at me so I could see the word and turned it
over and over again. He kept grinning at me but was always
focusing my attention on the word **"ESCAPE"**.

Suddenly he looked at the open sixth floor window
and made a dash for it. In a flash, I realised he intended to
jump out of the window. I dived for his legs. I got one hand
around his ankle just as he flew out into the open air. He
was too heavy and the force of his jump broke my grip.
When I looked out, he was a little more than half way down,
and still falling. He hit with a thud and bounced several feet
in the air. Bones, blood and tissue splattered everywhere!
His girlfriend came out of their bedroom and handed me a
stash of drugs and asked me to leave and would I please take
his drugs with me. She said, ' I called 911 and I don't want
them to find these. He's a schizophrenic. Didn't you
know?"

The next morning the lead story in the Long Beach
Newspaper concerned a young man who had leapt from a
building while high on LSD. This incident caused me to
question everything I had been doing. I was in shock for
months. The days of my holding the "pollyanna" belief that
drugs were a magical key to spiritual wisdom were over for
good. In this novella, I am attempting to deal with this
incident that happened a long time ago. If there is any

"good"news in this story it is that we can learn not to make the same mistakes over and over again.

Some people have said that this is a very dark story. I fully agree. It is. There was a dark side to the Age of Aquarius.

Table of Contents

Cover Art by Ellen Brouse

Short Stories:

A Novella:

Point to Point After

Zhen Hua's bookstore is located on the corner of
Franklin and East 13th Street and is within walking distance
of Oakland's little Chinatown district. A rectangular sign
hangs in the window and proclaims the store's function and
trade: "Books, bought and sold." On this particular day, a
Tuesday, Zhen was tending his shop. He was a slender man
weighing about one hundred and forty pounds. His face
was classically shaped and firm, for an older man, people
thought he radiated youth. When he entered the room,
everyone made way and let him pass. Even so, he was quiet
and unassuming, never given to imposing himself on others.
On this day, Zhen was putting the things in his shop in
order, and passing time to take his mind off his wife who lay
ill in bed.

As he works, a young man enters the shop setting
off a tiny bell. Zhen knows the boy is an aspiring writer
whose afternoons are often spent browsing used bookstores.
The boy is a favorite of Zhen's wife. Her interest in him
began when she discovered their shared love for poetry.
Zhen had often watched them as they passed entire
afternoons exchanging opinions and insights concerning the
nature of poetry and poetic truth. A strange empathetic

bond formed between his wife Leila and the young man. Zhen accepted this kinship knowing that it was innocent. It had in fact served to fire his interest in the boy.

"Good afternoon is Leila here?" The young man made his way directly to the counter opposite Zhen.

"No, I'm sorry, she hasn't been feeling well. Our Doctor has confined her to bed. Is there anything I can do for you?" Zhen replies, noticing that there are lines already forming in the corner of the boy's mouth. He wonders why this boy worries so much?

"Well I'm not sure, I brought her an article about the latest developments in computer art. I thought she might be interested." As was his custom the boy spoke deliberately picking each word with care.

"Ah yes, she mentioned a conversation with you, something about paintings that shift their line formations a thousand times per second, so fast that the mind's perception cannot keep up with the changes. No two patterns or drawings are ever the same."

"That's right, it's a new technique that shows vast improvement over earlier ones which were very clumsy. These have extremely complex color combinations, it has been described as a sort of universal looking glass made simple." The boy's calm demeanor is betrayed by unconscious twitches he makes at the corner of his mouth. Zhen takes note and thinks something is bothering this boy.

"You don't approve of this new blending of art and science?"

"Well I have mixed feelings, the pictures don't connect with me, they are robotic, they do not express feelings of any kind. How is Leila? Nothing serious I hope."

Zhen shifts his weight forward in his chair, his voice softens and he answers in a voice just above a whisper, "She is not well at all, the Doctor ran a series of tests last Friday. I'm going to go today to get the results. We're both past our primes, she's 58 and I'm 61. I don't want to take her with me this afternoon. If the news is really bad I want some time to figure out how to break it to her. She's had trouble before but I am afraid this may be the worst."

"I'm sorry to hear that, can I be of any help?" The boy's eyes glow with genuine concern.

"Would you mind staying with her this afternoon? She enjoys your company. It would be a relief for me to know you are with her." Zhen's request was honest; he would feel better if he knew Leila was not alone this afternoon.

"I'd be happy to."

Zhen walks out from behind the counter, his movements are quick and agile. He floats, giving the impression that his feet barely brush the ground. He closes the blinds and reverses the sign so that it now reads "CLOSED".

"It is nearly time for me to go, I hope you will not be inconvenienced." Zhen speaks over his shoulder as he locks the bolt on the front door. "You've been to our apartment before haven't you?"

"Yes. Several times."

"It is a blessing that you are here." Zhen motions to the boy to follow. He leads the young man through the empty store to the back door. Flicking off the light switch, he turns and surveys the room with a wistful look. His manner seems to say that something has been left undone, but he cannot remember what it is that he needs to do. A vacant look briefly crosses his face and is quickly gone.

"Oh, and one more thing, please don't mention any of our conversation to Leila. She doesn't know I am going to the Doctor. I don't know yet if there is any reason for concern and I don't want her to be alarmed."

"I understand," the boy nods in agreement.

Together the two men climb the stairs to the apartment above the store with the younger one following a step behind. The music of Mozart floats softly in the air. The stairs open into a familiar hallway where Zhen motions the boy to be seated in a small living room; he proceeds directly to a bedroom. The sounds of Mozart originate from this room.

"Leila, Dave has come to visit."

"The poet? I was hoping he would come, I have been thinking about him, I miss talking with him. " Zhen senses her mood has elevated. He motions the young man to enter.

"Hello Leila," Dave mumbles, shocked on seeing that Leila has become a wild eyed woman with her long hair knotted and twisted in a way he has never seen before. She seems dishevelled, less in control, it is not at all what he expected. A smile of recognition breaks across her face, she motions him to sit in an empty chair by the side of the bed.

"Hello David, what have you been doing?" he relaxes immediately, she has a way of putting him at ease. Her familiarity seems to form a bubble around them. Zhen lingers for a second in the doorway and then silently excuses himself, disappearing without saying a word. He is confident that she will not be distressed by his absence.

"I bought a magazine, it has an article about the new computer art. I have a new poem or two to show you as well." He holds out the magazine.

"I don't feel like reading, tell me what the article says." Dave senses that she is tired, and lacks her normal energy.

"It describes new techniques for subtle manipulations of form and color. The forms are consistent but the speed of the computer allows it to meld thousands of subtle changes, each faster than the eye can record or register."

Leila listens, but at the same time she gazes off into the distance. Her eyes are unfocused but they are not vacant. He knows she is looking at something but is at a loss to say what it is.

"Thousands of people, each different, thousands of lines, a million dots, different shades in a three dimensional matrix..." Leila's voice hangs in the air, erratic and scratchy...."crowds of people in the subway, each one pushing and shoving for space, for a tiny bit of room. When I was very young I lived in New York. I remember the sidewalks were so crowded, people spilled into the streets, the roads had gridlock, the cars could not move, yet still they did move, even if it was an inch at a time. A new art form. I imagine it will be popular, what do you think?"

"It lacks feeling. Who really cares? Art without feeling? How can that be art?" Dave made a face expressing disgust.

"That's what I thought you would say, have you ever been to New York? My family went there when we first came from China. The buildings are so close together, they often seem to touch each other, and they reach up so high they block the sky. The people are packed in even closer. Millions upon millions of people all different and yet all so similar. I used to ride the Staten Island Ferry every afternoon to get away from the crowds. The waves rocked the boat back and forth, it was so peaceful. It made me forget the crowds."

Zhen went through the kitchen and out the back door that opened on rickety old wooden stairs. Below in the alley his sixty-three Dodge sat parked in the afternoon sun. He turned on the radio and sat with the engine idling, he tried to collect his thoughts. His mind wandered ahead to the meeting at the Doctor's office where he hoped for some answers that would release the worry and tension that had been building inside. His hands nervously circled the wheel of the car as he pulled out onto the street.

Zhen imagined Leila staring blankly into space unaware of his presence in the room. Her periods of lost time were getting longer and more frequent. His mother had the same dull glaze in her eyes years before and he remembered it well. His mother's face haunted him, and now the same look was back but in Leila's face. He knew the condition was a loosening of mind. It had dominated the last years his family had spent together. It was a torturous time, some of the most difficult years of his life. In the end she did not know her own children.

He could hear her rambling recollections of Canton when its streets suddenly overflowed with the Japanese invaders who were bringing death to every corner. Each day she was tortured with the disappearance of her father, who was on his way home but never arrived. The fear and trembling would take over and occupy her mind making the memory seem real and as vivid as if it was once again the day it had all actually happened.

The possession always began with the hope that somehow he would avoid the thousands of troops who were killing every man in sight. She would wait, surely he would come, but he never did. Zhen's father had died, one of the many slaughtered that day. He was most likely buried in one of the huge fields where they hid the bodies of the crime. No one knew for sure.

It did not matter that decades had passed since the day of the crime and the world no longer remembered. Her fear had not passed, her trembling would never pass. She was trapped and she lived the horrors anew every day endlessly. The murdering rapists were always at the door even though no one was there.

After she became afflicted, these memories all returned and were vividly present. In the late stages of her disease, they took shape forming a collection of demons that she could not control. They were let loose daily to wreak havoc on those who loved her. Zhen snapped a left turn and rolled into the driveway of the downtown medical center. He parked the car and made his way to door number three in the complex.

"Good Afternoon, Mr. Hua, you're early." The receptionist gazed down at her logbook. "Have a seat, I'll let you know when the Doctor is available."

She vanished into one of the backrooms. A half hour later she called his name,"The Doctor will see you now."

As he waited, his mind broiled, reliving the horror of his mother's long passing from sanity. It was as if he were a baby held up by the ankles and redipped in the river that separates life from death. He felt as if he was being baptised in the transition his mother had made. It was as if a part of him had crossed when she crossed. He found himself praying and hoping that history was not about to repeat itself. He also soon found himself seated in a small interview room, waiting, once again he was waiting.

The door cracked open and Dr. Ming entered cautiously as if he were walking on eggshells, afraid he might break one. Zhen knew right away that the stone mask the doctor was attempting to wear meant bad news, very bad news. He listened as the doctor began to speak in a slow dull monotone. Zhen found himself tuning out the details, the doctors, what do they really know?

"... she has a tumor but she is also at the beginning of memory loss..... she will slowly begin to become disassociated from reality, familiar objects will become unfamiliar, she will not recognise old friends, time will become meaningless. Her mind may become erratic, she may suffer from irrational fears, at times she may not even know who you are. She may suffer physical pain but her anxiety may cause her to believe she is in pain even if she is not, imagined pain can seem as real as actual ailments." As Zhen looked at the Doctor he saw his mother just as she was at the very end when all was lost. He saw her expressionless smile flashing by in a long chain of endless blank stares.

"..the tumor is in a bad place, right behind her eye.. difficult to reach... difficult and dangerous to remove... rapid disintegration ... may be arrested... pain can be treated with opiates..." the Doctor's lips moved and the sounds came out.

Zhen heard him, or at least heard enough, yet somehow he could not respond except to nod his head occasionally. He felt like he was back sitting next to his mother's bed, the bed where she had pain for months, barely able to move, exhausted beyond caring. He saw the headboard with its carvings of the ancient Tao seeming to float in the air while framing her frail face. He recalled her ramblings, there had been opium then as well.

"How far along is it?" Zhen asked, though he knew she had already been ill for a while, too long he thought.

"It is a difficult thing to judge, there is no telling how long she has to live and what will happen exactly. I've contacted a specialist and will be turning this case over to him. The nurse has the details and will provide you with a referral."

"Pull the shades on the window, David, the sun is too bright." Dave moved to the window, drawing the blind and darkening the room. He resettled in the chair next to her bed.

"All of the furniture in this room looks to be hand carved. Do the carvings mean anything?"

"They represent the man-woman balance in the traditional taoist sense of life revolving endlessly between two poles. If you look closely you will see that the basic design follows a pattern of sorts. Each series tells a story, each is an episode from old mythology. All of this stuff belonged to Zhen's mother, they are all antiques."

Leila's voice quivered as she answered. Twisting, she pulled herself into a half sitting position with her feet dangling off the bed. She opened a bottle of pills and took two of them.

"They're painkillers, I will feel a bit better shortly."

"How did you and Zhen meet?" David had always been interested in their story but until now had not been able to ask for details.

"I came to California with my father. It was just the two of us. He was Chinese, born in the old country, he was not a wealthy man but he was very well educated. He taught school. We had enough of everything, I never really wanted for anything."

"How did you end up here in Oakland?"

"My mother was white, a missionary spreading the gospel in China. She died shortly after we returned to New York. I was very young. I have almost no memories of her." Leila began to rock to and fro in a gentle regular motion, her eyes shut. Her mind drifted back in time, she grabbed her knees steadying herself.

"Pull the blind daddy, I want to sleep." In her ears she could hear the wheels of the train rolling over the long line of tracks in the night. They were making the journey from New York to start life anew in California. Leila squinted up and saw her father's face looking at her, it was filled with joy and kindness. She remembered how handsome he had been.

"My Father did not like New York. When my mother died he got an offer in California, so we came west."

Gratitude filled Leila's being, gratitude that she could feel her father's presence once again. His elusive figure had returned clearly and it was reassuring.

"I forgot how much he cared. I can see him again in my mind's eye.." Leila smiled at David and fell asleep.

In her dream her father reaches out and touches her cheek, "You look just like your mother." She feels love and kindness flowing from his fingertips.

"How long has she been sleeping David?" Zhen is suddenly standing in the doorway.

"She took a couple of pills and dozed off about an hour ago." David is caught off guard, the older man appears without making a sound. "What did the Doctor say?"

"Nothing definite." Zhen put his finger to his mouth indicating they should be quiet. "Thank you for staying with Leila this afternoon. It was a big help to me." His voice is a quiet whisper. He motions Dave to join him in the kitchen.

"It was my pleasure to help, here is my phone number, if you need anything please don't hesitate to call me." David hands Zhen a sheet of notebook paper with his home details.

"Can I fix you a cup of coffee?" Zhen offers.

"No thanks, I have a couple of things to do this afternoon, I should be on my way." Zhen leads the young man to the backdoor, thanks him again and watches him disappear down the alleyway.

Zhen puts some water on the stove and sits down while waiting for it to boil. His mind churns as half buried thoughts and forgotten emotions swirl to the surface of his consciousness. He is rediscovering feelings he has not had for many years, and now they are suddenly fresh and raw. The long-buried past is resurrecting itself, bringing up memories that are decades old and making them seem new.

A loud gasp comes from the bedroom, he rushes in to find her sitting up in bed with her eyes wide open. She looks at him and it is as if he has been struck by a bolt of lightning. It hits him with hammer force and it seems as if a rush of clear light enters and overpowers his mind enveloping his entire being.

Zhen has a sense of falling headlong into the unknown. It is as if the room is being sucked into a tunnel, and his mind's eye is being forced to look inward. A sense of fusion lights every cell in his body and he becomes aware that Leila has joined with him. They are locked together swaying as if they are one pulse, one heartbeat, it is all a foggy haze but he knows and feels it is a union. They have joined together as one being.

He has a sense that they are whirling as if caught in a device that is circling madly. He feels they are pinned to a wall and the floor is being drawn away from beneath their feet leaving them suspended. Out of the darkness, visions come spinning, bringing into view clear, recognizable pictures of their mutually shared memories. Frozen moments now surfacing from the past as if they are alive and well and freshly formed.

He senses that some come from his mind and are his memories, but just as clearly he knows some are hers and come from her mind. They are entwined as if they are dancing together and falling in a spiral towards some base point that dances in their mutual matrix. He sees, then he becomes aware that she also sees, then they are aware that they see together, and finally they are aware that they are seeing through the same eye.

They have a view of each as they had once been, Leila is twenty-four and very beautiful as she makes her way down Fourth Street towards the outdoor marketplace in Oakland's Chinatown. She is humming softly as she picks her way through the crowd. Her large brown eyes are darting quickly, surveying and window shopping for fresh spices in the medicinal herb shop. She is interested in finding some fresh fo-ti which she thinks will bring her a sense of peace and well being.

 Zhen is coming up the same street from the opposite direction. He too is looking for fresh fo-ti, but in his case it is a tonic to keep a man virile and at the peak of manhood. He is twenty-seven, fresh out of graduate school and is meticulously dressed in a white shirt buttoned all the way to the top. His attire is finished off by a western style brown sport coat with matching slacks. He is humming a popular song and like her, is unaware that destiny is nearby. He enters the herb shop and heads for the bin where the fo-ti is kept. She is bent over the bin and is picking up a root when someone bumps her rudely from behind.

Annoyed, Leila looks up and into the eyes of Zhen for the first time. Each feels an immediacy, a warmth, a sense of familiarity and belonging that neither has ever felt before. It is as if a thousand greetings are exchanged in a matter of seconds without a word being spoken.

"Fo-ti is my favorite herb." She says not knowing what else to say. "It makes me feel calm and safe."

"I see, I have never heard that, it is said that it is a herb offering eternal vigor to men. I never knew women used it." Zhen smiled, "Is there enough for us both?"

"It appears there is a large quantity here, how much do you need to maintain your vigor?" she taunts him a little with a small wicked smile forming at the corner of her mouth.

"I am not sure, how calm are you?" he smiles back at her.

"A small quantity will do for me." she answers with another wicked smile.

Zhen knows that he has met the one he has been looking for, there is something saucy and independent about her that he likes. But does she feel the same?

Zhen realises that Leila is damp, dripping with sweat, seemingly unaware of her surroundings. She is half covered and only partly dressed in the old wooden bed. She has called to him and he has hurried to her side only to find her vacantly staring with empty lost eyes. Zhen undresses and joins Leila in the bed. She instinctively holds onto him, joining her body to him almost mechanically, their hands rubbing and searching for familiar lines of flesh that each knows by heart. Zhen feels her embrace him tightly, squeezing as if he is an anchor that will hold her in place, center her, and harbor her one more time. He accepts her knowing that this acceptance of each other is a temporary gift that he cannot expect to last forever. Soon there will be blind spots, and the blind spots will grow and become the normal state of things and then she will be lost to him. As this thought races through his mind, he holds her ever more tightly, as if to say, you will not get away.

They sit in a forty-two Ford high upon a hill watching the sunset behind the San Francisco city skyline. For a peaceful hour no word had passed between them, a temperate caressing breeze had been cooling them. Zhen has brought her here with a purpose, a mission, he has fallen so deeply for her that he needs to make it permanent.

"This is my favorite spot, it is so peaceful, do you feel it?" he finally breaks the long silence. "There is a sense of real peace here."

"It is calm here, nothing below seems to matter." She knows exactly what he means.

"I know we have only known each other a short time, but it feels as if we have always been together." Zhen speaks from his heart. "I think we should always be together."

"Are you saying you want to marry?" Leila is not surprised. It is what she wanted to hear.

"Yes, that is what I am saying." He takes her in his arms and kisses her. They make love as the night falls, it is as if they are the only ones in the entire world, and the whole of eternity has opened its arms for them.

Zhen wakes in the old wooden bed with Taoist carvings
lying next to the sleeping body of his wife. A look of sweet
pain is flowing across Leila's face, it makes her seem both
young and old at the same time. A murmur, a deep sigh
sounds from deep inside her chest and it shakes her. Zhen
brushes her hair from her face and with an unconscious
gesture he kisses her shoulder. She shudders as if something
cold has touched her. She opens her eyes and looks at him
with horror.

"I am losing you, I will soon be gone, and will not know
you." Her eyes are full of fear and at the same time hold a
desperate longing, she wants things to stay, to be as they
once were. "Do not let me go." She pleads.

They cross a narrow bridge that spans two banks of a wide
river flowing below on its journey to the sea. Moonlight
reflects and shimmers in ever changing patterns making the
river seem unreal and far away. A thin covering of moisture
serves as a lubrication allowing their locked bodies
movement as they hold each other ever more tightly.

"Never let me go." It is not clear whose voice said it.
Neither of them can be sure. Zhen's hand feels for the
drawer and he finds what he is looking for, he knows he has

to do it. "We will go together." In their dream two eagles soar away together rising in the currents of the night air in a perfect spiral towards an inner sun. Far below limp and listless their bodies are lifeless, lying in pools of blood on the bed.

Dave, the poet, wakes a bit after ten. It is later than is his norm, he puts on an old pair of trousers and a dirty shirt. Thoughts of Leila and Zhen are foremost in his mind. He is worried, he cannot shake or explain his thoughts. Surely they belong together if anyone ever did, why should he worry, they would find a way. He washes the sleep from his eyes and goes to get his morning paper.

It seems like an invisible hand is turning the pages of the paper to section B page thirteen where he sees a caption: "Murder, Suicide in Oakland."

"Early this morning police were called by neighbors to the residence of Zhen Hua a prominent bookseller. Fearing that a robbery had taken place, police entered and found the couple in bed, each with a bullet wound in the middle of their foreheads. Foul play has been ruled out, Mr. Hua seems to have killed his wife and then taken his own life. An investigation is in progress, anyone with information relating to this matter is encouraged to contact the police."

"Blind San Franciscans"

It was late afternoon and Don was alone in his office on the corner of 7th and Market Street. It was an old building in dire need of maintenance. His office was on the fifth floor of the fifteen story structure. The rents were dirt cheap. His was the only unit in use on the fifth floor, all the others were empty. Some were boarded up.

Don was experiencing the onset of middle age, it was a fight he was losing. He went to the gym often but that was only delaying the inevitable. He had been gradually losing his hair so rather than wait for it to all fall out he shaved his head bald. In spite of his various aging issues, some thought he was an attractive man. A few even compared him to Yul Brenner. It was a comparison he liked.

He stood there staring at a pile of recently sealed envelopes that needed to be mailed. He had addressed them by hand. It was a tedious job, one that he did every day. It always made him think, "I really should not have to do the mundane tasks like this." The job took anywhere from an hour to three hours to do. It all depended on how many orders had been written the night before. Today the job took most of the morning. Life was good.

"Gold, pure gold," he muttered to himself, "Who else could do this? Start something from scratch? And make it pay off in spades."

Don liked the life he was leading, he was getting respect and he loved it. It had been a hard road. Things hadn't always been so sweet. It was a mere four years since his fall from grace. How did it happen? In retrospect he blamed his own stubbornness. It was his refusal to compromise along with his rigid desire to do what was right. He had to admit that he was bull headed.

He had been a rising star in a San Francisco ad agency when he discovered that his biggest client was using him to commit fraud. He tried to expose them, but was stopped dead in his tracks. Instead of exposing them, he ended up being blackballed throughout the industry. He was branded as being a man who could not be trusted with secrets. He soon found himself alone and on the street.

In a flash, he went from being flush with cash to being nearly penniless and unemployable. His attempt to expose his client's malfeasance was worse than the crime being committed. The "code" required him to look the other way.

He floundered, but then in a flash of inspiration he found a way to put his talents to work. He started over and in a short time things began to turn around. He had a vision! It was one of sweeping magnitude! He suddenly knew how to tap into the best instincts of people and use them to his advantage.

Almost overnight he became the very symbol of what a "good" man should be, it was a part he played very well. He created a charity, and became the benefactor of the blind, and by doing so he was fast becoming rich again. He gathered up the stack of envelopes and hurried off to the post office to send the missives out into the world to work their magic. They were the key to the incoming cash flow that he was now enjoying so much.

One by one his work crew straggled in and took their places. Most of them were down and out. They were disenfranchised. They were the hangers on! Some were living on the streets, others were just a step away from life without a roof.

A few of them were young and still had energy and life in their steps. Those few were his "top producers" but they were rare. Most of his "people" had been knocked around and had fallen into the cracks of society. They were constantly looking over their shoulders, expecting the hand of doom to descend from out of nowhere and crush them as it always had.

There were nearly equal numbers of men and women and they were all down on their luck. The group chatted among themselves and waited quietly for Don to give the signal to begin. They were all veterans of the process and knew the drill. Don surveyed the room. It was nearly full which gave him great satisfaction. The cash register was going to ring again tonight. He could hear it going ka-ching! He always wanted to fill every desk, but that was rarely possible. Tonight he had a good crew. He could tell they were anxious to get started. They all needed the cash he paid nightly.

"Begin!" he yelled out the command while holding up a small wind-up alarm clock that showed it was exactly six o'clock. The rag tag band of telemarketers began instantly to dial the phones which were now ringing in homes all over the city.

"Keep at it! Dial those phones! We are coming up to show time! Sell those tickets!"

Every phone was in hand and up to the ear of its user. They were reading the script and writing orders all over the room. Don got out his little black ledger book and checked off the attendance of each person who had shown tonight. He prepared enough cash envelopes to pay the group. Everything was done on a first name basis. He kept track of their attendance and accumulated outgoing sales on a night by night basis. When the shift ended he would give each one a little cash packet containing $7.00. It was their pay in full for three and a half hours.

"Hey! What the hell are you two doing back there? No chit chat allowed, I'm not running a social club, get to work or I'll separate you."

Don got up and made a gesture towards a couple in the back of the large workroom. The object of Don's anger was a young man named Bob. Bob looked up with fiery eyes and glared back at him. The young woman he was flirting with kept her head down and refused to acknowledge there was a problem.

They were his two top producers. They were unusual. Bob had a day job and was here picking up extra cash. Joan was in college and seemed well enough off. "Damn fine phone voices, both of them" he thought, and they have great personalities in their phone presentations.

Don got up and stood behind Bob's chair and looked over his shoulder. There were stacks of new orders piled in front of both of them already. Bob had sold four books of tickets and Joan was writing her fourth as he watched.

"I'm going to have to move you to another spot." He put his hand on Bob's shoulder and gave him a little jerk. "You're too distracted."

"Hell I am, no!" Bob reacted by moving his shoulder violently. The force of his shoulder jerk threw Don's hand off into the air "I ain't movin! I already sold four sets of tickets. Nothing is holding me back."

Don backed off. He hadn't expected Bob's anger. Joan looked at him with pleading eyes. "Leave us alone."

Don spoke loudly in a voice calculated to make sure everyone in the room heard.

"Alright, talk a little less to her and a little more to them out there. They're all waiting to hear from you, they all want to donate! Don't waste time! The blind are depending on you! Sell tickets! Raise money! Sell! Sell! Sell!"

Don backed off and made his way around the room encouraging each one to call with gusto, "turn em and burn em", "Sell those tickets". "The time to give is now, donate and come to our big variety show." His voice thundered out filling the room.

He returned to his table to see a young woman with a backpack and sleeping bag enter the room. She seemed frightened and looked timidly around the room. She was short and slender with close cropped red hair and bangs partially covering her eyes.
Don approached her. Her eyes flashed revealing a crystal clear blue stare, and then she quickly looked away down at the floor. She is young, very young he thought.

"How old are you?" he asked, worrying that she might be a minor.

She didn't respond. Her eyes began to wander about the room jumping from desk to desk. She had never seen a telephone boiler room before and had no idea what to think.

"Over here." Don called out to her. "You looking for a job?"

She nodded shyly "yes".

She could not engage with Don. Instead, she focused on two broken windows covered with cardboard. The dingy dirty room had her spellbound. Her eyes found the cobwebs hanging in the corners of the room and finally her survey found the bare electric bulbs dangling from the ceiling. All the while dozens of voices were repeating the same sales script over and over, droning on in unison. Her mind reeled.

"Yes, but I didn't expect..." her voice trailed off and she was unable to finish the sentence.

"This is a charity outfit, no frills, no wasted money! What's your name?" Don's bald head glared and shined beneath the bright bulbs.

"May, " she answered. She thought he looked wolfish and was intimidated by his stare.

"Well May, if you want a job read this over and then recite it out loud like I was a customer on the phone. Treat it like you were giving a speech in school." He thrust a mimeographed paper into her hands. She took it and read it over. Don watched her closely.

"Easy isn't it?" He asked. She nodded yes, "Good now read it to me." She began trying to read the compact little presentation.

"We are San Franciscans for the blind. We are calling to ask you to buy tickets to our first annual variety show. The proceeds will go to fund college scholarships for the blind."

She fumbled with the paper and stuttered a bit. She got frustrated and quit. Don shook his head and clicked his teeth.

"Not bad, there's more, you got to tell them the price and the dates." He looked sternly at her. "You always have to close by asking them to buy the tickets. They won't do it if you don't push them."

"I don't know if I can call people, I don't know." She was flustered. The ad she had answered did not say much other than there was a nightly payout for three and a half hours work. Two dollars an hour, leave tonight with cash in hand!

"You got to talk louder and be more friendly. Let the warmth and kindness come out of your voice. You are representing a good cause. Let them know how much good work their buying tickets will do. Sell them goodness and charity. Let them hear it in your voice."

"Give me another chance, I need the job." She pleaded child-like. "I'll get it, you'll see."

"Sure you will honey. Try it again."

Don had two empty desks. He always gave everyone a second chance. He paid minimum wage, in cash. All they had to do was sell four tickets and his payroll costs were covered.

When asked, he always said it was a numbers game.

"Make thirty calls an hour for three hours and you are a sure thing to sell four tickets. Just put your head down and keep dialing"

As a special incentive, he paid a ten dollar cash bonus when a salesperson billed out a total of 100 tickets. Don kept the sales records in his little book.

May started reading again. She stopped and started, and lept fumbling the lines, but she read the whole thing.

"Don't worry about it, You'll be a pro in no time. Sit at that empty table in the back. Here are some pages out of the phone book. Call line by line. When you get a "yes" you write up the order on this little three by five card. Confirm their name and address before you hang up. The tickets are three dollars each so a book of four is $12.00. Tell them the price as we are going to mail them an invoice. They get the tickets when they pay. Try to sell no less than two tickets per order. I don't like singles. Go ahead and start calling."

"Thanks mister, I know I can do it and I need money real bad. I haven't eaten today."

"Yeah okay, get to work, the night is nearly half gone. You got two hours left to call. You can still make $4.00 tonight."

May took phone numbers and called her first prospective donor. "Sweet kid" he thought, and went back to supervising the crew.

Joan leaned over and poked Bob in the ribs.

"She is awfully young." She nodded at the newcomer.

"Yeah, he never checks I.D's. or takes any information about anyone he hires, doesn't take social security numbers, pays cash and is always here by himself." Bob had suspicions for a while. He kept his voice down trying to avoid detection.

"I wonder about him, what's he getting out of this?" Joan gave Bob a look that said she too wanted answers. "How can we find out?"

"I don't know. Why do you care?"

"When I answered the job ad I thought it was for charity, but the more I watch and listen to Don, the less I believe in it." She finished writing her seventh order of the night. She was two behind Bob for the night.

She kept track of who wrote the most orders. They always sat next to each other and she was competing with him. It was a fact that had not yet dawned on Bob.

"I am not sure, there must be something, a business license, something we could check to see what is really going on."

"I am going to go by the auditorium where the show is going to be staged tomorrow. It is out near the Cow Palace, down in the South City. Wanna go with me and see what is there?"

"Really? Sure. How can we get there?" Like most people in the city, he did not have a car.

"There's a bus that stops every hour at Van Ness and Market and it goes right by there." Joan had done her research.

"Great, let's do it." Bob was ecstatic, it was his chance to see her out of work. He had been trying to figure out a way to make that happen. Here it was. Gift wrapped, a date, or sort of a date.

"Okay, tomorrow at noon at the corner stop". She went right back to work.

"Hello, this is Joan from the Blind San Franciscans calling to let you know about our variety show. It is coming up on June 10 and all proceeds from the show will go to a scholarship fund for the blind. How many tickets can I send you? They are $3.00 each, how many do you want?" She paused and was rewarded. She made another sale.

"You'll take four? Wow, that's great! Are you still living at 111 Pine Street, unit 15? We'll send you the invoice in the mail along with a stamped return envelope. You'll get the tickets when you pay the invoice..Enjoy the show and the blind thank you!"

The night ground on and both Bob and Joan wrote order after order. They were smooth and polished and they found most people wanted to help.

"It's 9:30, quitting time."it was Don's voice cutting loudly through the buzz. All activity ceased immediately. "Stop! No calls after 9:30."

"Bring your orders as always, I've got your nightly envelopes. Bob has written over a 100 orders, everybody let's all give Bob a round of applause. He gets the $10.00 bonus tonight!"

Bob turned in index cards for twenty two tickets sold and took his pay envelope. It contained the extra ten dollars and he was happy. Joan had sold twenty six. She had gotten a hot streak and passed Bob during the last hour of the night.

"Bob is well on his way to a second hundred, and Joan is really close!" Don announced their totals and everyone marvelled at their success. "Keep coming back to work, I like giving out the bonus!"

May had sold only six tickets. When she turned in her total, Don asked her to stay after work for a talk. The room emptied and they were alone.

"I know I can do better, just give me another chance." May's voice quivered in anticipation.

"I think so too. I want you to come back tomorrow. I am going home to a late supper. Since you haven't eaten today I was wondering if I could get you to join me? I have a cab waiting downstairs. Would you like some supper?" He gave her a piercing stare.

May took the little envelope he offered containing her $4.00 for the night. She was hungry, very hungry, it had been two days since she had eaten and the offer for supper was welcome. The big, bulky balding man smiled at her and she decided she was too hungry to say no, besides she was thankful the door was still open and she needed to work again.

"Sure, sounds great." She accepted despite the little voice telling her that it was unwise to go to a strange man's house alone.

In the elevator Don towered above her. He was a full foot taller than she was. He was pushing two hundred and twenty pounds. She was a little over a hundred dripping wet and naked. She tried to guess how old he was." I'll bet he's over forty" was her best guess. She didn't have the nerve to speak to him about it. She thought "He might even be older than that".

"There's the cab, waiting just like I said. I live up in Pacific Heights. It is ten minutes away at this time of night." Don opened the door for her and helped her get in the back seat.

May wedged up against the door putting her sleeping bag and backpack between them. She looked out the window as it wound its way to an exclusive part of town. The cab stopped in front of a mansion with a panoramic view of the San Francisco bay.

"You live here?" The house was an enormous two story Victorian in perfect condition with a long balcony and a large yard, surrounded by an iron fence with a well hedged walkway that led up to a porch with a swinging love seat suspended from the ceiling.

"Yes, the house is a holdover from better days. I am trying to keep it going."

The entrance foyer had a coat closet. Don hung his coat and offered to take hers. Suddenly May was aware that there were other people in the house.

"You home Don? The stew is ready to be served." A voice floated in from the interior of the house.

"Yeah and I have a dinner guest. Put out an extra place." Don responded. "We're having Beef Bourguignon tonight. Frederick is an excellent cook and it is one of my favorites. Do you likc it?"

"Uh, I don't know, what is it exactly?" May was overwhelmed. She felt a rush of relief, thank god she thought "there are other people in the house."

"It's pretty easy to make. Very tender beef with garden vegetables and a fantastic broth. We usually have sourdough with it. The dining room is to the left, the washroom is to the right, if you want to clean up." Don gestured in both directions and she went to wash up.

The bathroom was an elegant room with hand towels put out for individual use, "like a hotel" she thought. The fixtures were expensive porcelain and the hand soap sat in a shell-like dish. She washed and gathered herself and went to dinner. To her amazement the dining room had a long oak dining table surrounded by a dozen matching chairs. Nearly every chair was filled, with people busy chatting and laughing. It was a lively group, and all eyes turned on her when she entered the room.

"What do you do my dear?" a tail thin man with a goatee wearing a flowing long sleeved white shirt with elegant ruffles asked her.

"What do you mean?" May was intimidated.

"Well, what kind of an act do you do? I recite Shakespeare. What do you do?" His eyes were intense and piercing.

"This is Frederick, he was tonight's chef and is also an actor." Don introduced the speaker.

"We're all performers," an overweight woman in a granny dress chimed in. "I'm Lorraine, I do magic and conduct seances ." "Stella there is a singer, mostly opera and show tunes. That's Jason, he is a juggler, fire sticks and chain saws. Michael is a puppet master. Everyone does something, what do you do?"

"Well, I just met Don. I read the script for a while tonight. I'm homeless."

"I invited her to come eat with us. She has gone hungry for a few days." Don answered and nodded at Lorraine indicating she should back off." Take a piece of bread and dig in." May took his advice and scooped a bowl full of stew and began to eat.

"We all perform at the wharf and the square all day. I have the corner right in front of the chocolate factory. Stella is on the wharf right by the wax museum.' Lorraine kept right on talking ignoring Don's silent request to be silent. "Everyone has a special talent, you just haven't found yours yet."

Lorraine went for a share of the Bourguignon and started eating.

"Well, I do dance a little." May said sheepishly.

"Exotic?" It was Frederick chiming in.

"No, modern. It's just a hobby."

"Well, I'd like to see you dance." Don jumped in. "Maybe you could dance in the show. Let me explain when my mom died I inherited this big house. Then I lost my job and had all these empty rooms. I began boarding people, Frederick was my first."

"I was reciting bits of Shakespeare on the street by Ghirardelli square and taking collections from the crowds." Frederick jumped in telling his story.

"He was struggling. He had only a tiny income, but I gave him a room. He was the first to start living here with me."

"Once I saw how big this house was and how empty, I introduced Lorraine to Don, she often worked a spot near me on the street." Frederick continued.

"The next thing I knew I had a house full of street artists living here helping to pay my mortgage. These are the people who are going to put on the show we are selling tickets for. They're the stars." Don looked from face to face and smiled at his band of stage warriors.

May sized them all up. They all seemed friendly and kind. She relaxed. "Wow! I had no idea."

"We've all been homeless or close to it." It was Jason, the juggler. "We've all been where you are at now."

"Do you need music to dance? What kind of music do you like to dance to? I play the piano, and Stella sings. My name is Michael. "If you would like to dance for us, we'll back you up."

"Let me think about it." May ate and listened to the conversations in awe. She really liked to dance. She had been so busy trying to survive, she had thought of nothing else. Dancing was a hobby. She wondered, could it be something more? Lately her main concern was finding a place to stay. She felt that she had slept in the park long enough. Was dancing the answer to her woes? It seemed crazy.

As the dinner went on May got to know a little about each
of the artists who were sitting at the table sharing bread with
her. They put her at ease and made her feel at home. The
one thing she noticed most was that they all deferred to Don
and they all seemed to like him. He began to look less
wolfish and more benign. She started to think he might even
be handsome in a rugged sort of way. He made jokes and
laughed and finally he looked directly at her and spoke.

"We have an empty room here. If you want you can stay the
night." He asked her without any hint of force. It was
clearly her choice.

"Yes, I am very tired of Golden Gate park." May accepted,
grateful for the providence fate was providing.

"Good, we always have a couple of glasses of port after
dinner, do you want one?" Don said changing the subject.

She had a glass of port and then another. Michael started
playing the piano, and he was very good at it. She knew the
music he was playing by heart. It vibrated in her body and
she felt like dancing.

"I will dance for you if you like." The port had made her warm and floaty. She was happy and at home. She felt great.

"Sure, please do," Don and the group cleared some room in the living room.

May stripped down to her underwear and bra, and stretched to limber her arms and legs. Her body was curvy and slim. She started slowly doing some basic reaches and jumps extending her arms and legs in graceful lines.

"She moves like an angel." Frederick muttered to Don under his breath.

The pace of the music quickened and she felt a stirring in her body. The rhythms were sensual and flowing. She felt free and wild. Her dancing projected an image of sweetness and sexual longing. Her body was becoming wet and damp as if she was soaking in a steamy sultry heat. She pounced and slipped from spot to spot covering the entire room.

She was transformed and until her body became nothing but flowing perfect lines moving gracefully in the night. The room was silent. She was in her own world of dance, and it was as if no one else existed at all. It was just the piano and her pulsing, jumping nearly naked self filling time and space with magic. She kept on improvising, with her body speaking in a language without words for a full ten minutes. Beads of water formed on her back and rolled between her buttocks. She glistened and gathered her audience's attention until they were wrapped in her web of moving body parts. She created a cocoon of shelter, amazement and delight.

Then suddenly she stopped and bowed her head! The music stopped as well and the room was completely silent.

"Yes, you can dance." Lorraine broke the silence clapping. They all clapped and acknowledged the moment.

May got dressed.

"How about another drink?" Don opened another bottle of port and poured a round for everyone.

"You should do a bit in our show." Lorraine said excitedly while drying May's dripping back.

"Yeah I loved it, you should dance in the show." Michael chimed in.

They quickly finished the bottle of port and were soon consuming another. The conversation centered around the upcoming variety show and how much they each looked forward to being a part of it. Underneath the conversation there was an unspoken awareness that May had introduced a sensual bonding into the group that had never been there before.

"The empty room is on the second floor right across from the master bedroom. Lorraine will show it to you if you like." Don gestured that it was late and time to turn in. " I have room for one more." Don watched May's athletic body climb the stairs and thought, she's not such a lost child after all.

Bob approached the corner stop at Market and Van Ness at 11:45. He was early. He did not want to miss his big chance. Since he had met her, he was finding it difficult to think of anyone else. Joan was not there. A rag lady was lying on the bench with her eyes closed. He checked the schedule posted by the bench, the S44 was due at twelve exactly. That had to be the bus. He saw Joan crossing the street against the traffic light.

"Hi." Bob smiled at her.

"Thanks for coming. The bus runs along Mission down the south of market for a mile and then heads down to the south city. That part of town is really tough. I didn't want to be alone." Joan smiled back.

"No problem, did you say the event is being held at the Cow Palace, that's a huge place. I went there for a rodeo once." Bob commented.

"Nah, it's a place near the Cow Palace. An old movie theater." Joan answered.

"What do you expect to learn?"

"Well, I want to see if there are advertisements for the show. Get an idea what the venue is like? How big is it? What does the neighborhood look like? What are we selling?" Joan gave Bob a shrug of her shoulders.

The S44 arrived on time, they paid their fares and boarded. Joan took the window seat.

"This is a long ride. The bus stops a lot." She gave Bob a serious piercing look. "Don seems so greedy. He is a harsh man. I have a hard time seeing him do anything for charity. He just doesn't seem like the type."

"Yeah, I get that." Bob knew she was right about Don. He was pushy and demanding. At times Bob had found himself questioning whether there was actually a variety show being produced at all. Were there really scholarships for blind people? Why was Don always alone? Was there anyone else involved with the Blind San Franciscans? "Sometimes it seems like he is a one man operation."

"Yeah, I think he might be." Joan nodded in agreement. "I didn't sign up to do this because I need the money. I wanted to do something good. Something pure and I just don't feel like that is what is happening. Why are you doing it?"

Bob needed the money. He thought about what to tell her. He decided to tell her the truth.

"I broke up with a girl I was living with and had to start over. It was sudden. I got caught short of money. I found a day job but the search took weeks. I won't get my first paycheck until the end of this week. I been getting by on the cash Don pays."

"I see. Was your girlfriend paying all your bills?"

"We were sharing expenses but I had to get an apartment and that cost money upfront. I was scraping by. The day I graduated from college she called it quits. It was sudden. I ended up out on the street."

"She broke up with you?" Joan asked.

"Yeah, caught me by surprise. I didn't have any cash saved, so I need this gig. I am eating off the cash. I am getting back on my feet." The whole discussion made Bob queasy.

"I understand. I'm seeing a married man. First time I ever did anything like that." Joan answered.

"Is it serious?" Bob was disappointed.

"It is for me. He is separated. He wants to get back with her but can't. She won't take him back. I really like him." Joan averted her eyes.

"I get it sort of. I don't really feel single." Bob had hoped to avoid talking about his past. "It just happened."

"I guess we are both in shaky places. I am interested in a person who is not really feeling the same way and so are you."

"I am getting over a two year relationship." Bob was disappointed Joan was attached. " I feel betrayed."

They both withdrew into quiet thought. The bus passed through the spanish section of San Francisco and into South San Francisco. South City contained the few remaining manufacturing sites still operating on the peninsula. It was dotted with factories and rows of warehouse buildings. Off to Bob's left the dock areas rolled by.

"That's Pier 96. They have the only container cranes in San Francisco.." Bob pointed to the large cranes trying to make conversation.

"The Cow Palace is coming up. We'll get off there and I think the theater is two blocks east towards the bay." Joan broke her long silence. "Sorry to hear about the trouble with your girlfriend, that's too bad."

"Yeah, I'm getting over it." Bob looked away.

"I called the theater. I got an answering machine and no one returned my call. I left a couple of messages. I looked up the address on my map of the city."

They found the theater building. It was closed. The marquee was advertising "The Graduate" with Dustin Hoffman. The sign was at least two years out of date. The place was deserted. It must have been closed for a long time.

"Nothing going on here." "Are you sure this is the place?" Bob asked.

"Yeah I'm sure. There's nothing posted about a variety show. It looks like this place hasn't been open for years." Joan agreed.

"Nothing posted about anything. I saw the Graduate two years ago, good movie, looks like it was their last show here. At least it was a good one."

"It explains why no one returned my calls." Joan looked upset. "What do you think we should do now?"

"I don't know. What is the explanation?The variety show is a month away. Maybe they're planning on cleaning it up and re-opening it."

"Maybe, they better get started soon. Who's gonna do it? Don spends all his time raising money and selling tickets." Joan's voice was hypercritical. Bob could tell she was convinced there was no show planned for this theater.

"I don't like what I am seeing," he said. Joan nodded her head in agreement.

"Let's think about it. I am not sure what is the best way to move." Bob had no idea what to do.

The bus ride back passed in silence. Bob had hoped to get something romantic started with Joan. It hadn't turned out that way yet. They arrived back at Van Ness and market and as they got off the bus Joan remarked, " I think we may be participating in a fraud. Maybe we are ripping people off."

"Maybe, I hope not. Do you want to confront Don?"

"I don't think it would do any good. He'd just fire us. We need some hard evidence. Some proof." Joan answered.

"Okay. Any idea on what that might be?"

"Not yet. You are going to work tonight?" Joan asked

"Yeah, I really have to for the rest of this week. I have no money till I get my first check."

"Okay, I'll see you tonight."

Lorraine reached out and took May's damp arm and patted her hand.

"You're limp. Like a little rag doll. Come with me and I'll get you settled in."

May was indeed exhausted from her dancing outburst and was thankful for the help. Lorraine led her to the stairs and helped May to the door to the one bedroom that was available for an overnight guest.

"See you in the morning. We share the bathroom right down the hall."

May curled up in the cool soft sheets and slept without fear or anxiety for the first time in weeks. It was a new and strange environment but she felt no fear. She knew she would not be rousted by the patrolling park police tonight. She slept until after nine and might have slept longer if Lorraine had not come to give her a last call for breakfast.

"Sweetie, we have some eggs and toast ready if you're hungry."

May opened her eyes and looked around the room. She had fallen asleep quickly and not had the energy or the interest to really take note of where she was. Sleeping in the park had been difficult. The park police were a threat to arrest her at any time. She was young and beautiful. It made her a target for some of the homeless men. She knew a few of them were dangerous, and was always on her guard ready to fight off an attacker. Sleeping for her consisted of napping with one eye open.

"That sounds lovely. I'll be right down." Breakfast was a delicious luxury.

Frederick was waiting with two eggs in one hand and a frying pan in the other.

"How do you like your eggs? Toast and jam, coffee and cream are right there ready. The eggs will take a minute." He smiled and nodded to the food.

"Over easy, sunny side up! Do you do all the cooking?" remembering he had made the stew the night before.

"A lot of it, I liked your dance, have you ever thought of trying to combine it with mime?" I think if you worked at it, you could do a combination of dance and mime. Wear white face and gloves, get a pants suit, people would stop and watch. You'd make money. You should think about it."

"Mime, I saw it done once. Yeah that's a thought." It was a thought May had never had before, but she let it begin to sink in.

"All of us entertain the tourists, nearly everyday. A lot of people visit San Francisco. I pull in $50.00 some days and Lorraine with her magic show does better. There's no one doing mime right now."

"Sounds like fun. Have you lived here long?"

"Nah , I moved in two months ago. Don saw me perform and Don took me in. I was broke. He had this big house, all alone, needed help with the bills,I started cooking and paid what I could, one thing led to another, I spread the word, and now we are all together like a big family."

"Wow. Last night it seemed like you all knew each other forever." May said, amazed.

"We knew each other from our gigs! Most of us have been working on the streets for a while." Frederick answered.

"The variety show? What about that? Is that brand new then?"

"Don came up with the idea last month."

"Wow just like that," she snapped her fingers.

Lorraine came into the room dressed in a flowing gown with pictures of stars and crescent moons covering it. She sat next to May and reached out and took her hand.

"What have you got planned for today." She asked.

"Nothing. It's been awhile since I had anything planned."
May answered.

"Why don't you come with me today and watch me work at
the wharf. Get an idea on what it is like." Lorraine smiled
warmly.

"Sure, I'd like that."

"I make sandwiches everyday. There's a pile of them in the
fridge. Take what you think you'll need." Frederick chimed
in. "I told her she should think about becoming a mime.
Combine it with her dancing."

"That is a great idea." Lorraine nodded her head yes and
squeezed May's hand tightly. "Spend the afternoon with me.
The wharf will be packed. You'll see what it is about."

"You really think I could make enough to get by being a
mime and dancing?"

"Yeah I think so, but watch and learn. Tonight go to work with Don. You should move in with us. Don wants you to."

"You think so?" May asked.

"Sure, we all had problems when we moved in here. Just ask Don. The answer will be yes. He's a good man."

The door to the headquarters of the Blind San Franciscans was locked tight. Don was late and the crowd of workers was gathering anxiously in the hallway. Bob was the first to arrive. He read a book and waited patiently for Joan. He wondered if she would come since the trip to the theater. They were both convinced the variety show was a hoax.

The elevator bell rang. Its door opened and Joan walked into the hallway. She saw Bob jammed in the back of the group against the halfway wall. She sidled up next to him.

"He must be late." her voice was agitated.

"Yeah. How was your day?"

"I did some research on charities. They have to be registered with the state to be legal.I called Sacramento and they didn't have any papers for Blind San Franciscans."

"That's bad." Bob saw the look of anger in her eyes. What was she going to do now?

"They said if it is really new it could still be in process." She shrugged her shoulders."I am not sure if I want to confront Don or go straight to the authorities and let them deal with it."

"What good will it do to confront him?" Bob asked.

"Well, maybe he has an answer to my questions."

"No matter what, I think he will be unhappy." Bob answered. "He won't react well."

Just as he spoke, the elevator door opened and Don and May came out together. Don swaggered up and unlocked the front door. May followed close behind and took the desk next to him. She sat close to him.

"We have minutes to get ready to work. Sorry I am a bit late, but it won't matter. We can get in a full night's work." Don yelled out instructions and took little packets of "call" pages and scurried around the room giving each person their numbers for the night,

 "It's six o'clock! Get to work."

Every desk sprang into action and the calling began. Don recorded the night's attendance and prepared his "pay" packets.

Joan did nothing.She picked up her phone and started dialing. After a minute she put it down.

"It looks like she is with him now. There must be thirty years between them. She's way too young for him." Joan nodded toward May. "Unbelievable"

"Yeah, he kept her late last night and now they show up late together. I think she is homeless."

"I can't do this anymore. It's too much. What a sleeze.He is too much. I am going to the authorities." Joan gathered up her stuff and walked out the door without saying a word to Don.

Don watched the scene unfold. His top producer left in an angry huff. He walked over to Bob's spot to investigate.

"What's going on?" he asked Bob.

"She left." Bob answered.

"I know that. I see that. Why?" Don pushed for an explanation.

"Uh, she checked with the State and they had no record of a charity called The Blind San Franciscans. Did you file papers with them?" Bob spoke without making eye contact.

"She checked our registration?" he looked bewildered.

"Yeah I guess she did." Bob responded.

"Well I'll be damned. Why?"

"Tell me, how many scholarships are we offering and how big are they?"

"Too early to say, ask me after we have finished selling tickets." Don shrugged his shoulders as if to say "what next, you can't please everybody." and walked off.

"Keep dialing those phones, people want to "give" and we want them to donate. Dial! Dial! Dial!" Don's big voice boomed across the room. Bob went back to work. He needed the money.

The Cat Burglars

"Man, I'm the best." Lee leaned back in his chair tilting it away from the mirror he was looking in. His young voice exuded masculinity and power. He felt important. He was getting somewhere in life. Mark had acknowledged him and asked him to his apartment. It was the first time he had been invited to Mark's place. It was impressive, a top floor unit with wide expansive windows looking out at the San Francisco bay.

"You're full of shit." Mark replied. He thought of Lee as strictly small-time. Lee had badgered him with attempt after attempt to join forces and partner up. Out of curiosity he had decided to look him over but he knew deep down it would never work out. He had best keep to himself. The less anyone knew his business the better. Mark put down the newspaper he was reading and focused on Lee.

"It's true and you know it. Hands down I'm the best and that's a fact" Lee kept up the bravado. The swagger in his voice was equaled only by the swagger in his step.

"The way you stare at yourself in the mirror, I'd say you're in love." Mark was having none of it. "I cleared three g's this week and I was taking it easy. Being loud and cocky has nothing to do with how good you are."

"Talk is cheap, I've never seen you work. As far as I know it's all talk." Lee pushed back at Mark.

They had known each other for over a year having met while fencing hot goods. Over time they had become "friends". The truth was Lee longed to partner with Mark. Mark had the reputation and the money. The style and elegance of the penthouse he lived in attested to that. As they say, he thought, money talked and he has got it big time.

"I always work alone, safer that way. I told you many times how I feel." Mark had resisted Lee's request that they become a team. Alone, he could control every detail, but with a partner he knew he became vulnerable. If a partner made a mistake, it was his problem.

"Yeah well I think that's bull shit. I don't think you can hold a candle to me." Lee challenged him again.

"I had a good friend, never made a mistake. Every job was clean and he was never caught. Then one night he took someone along. Next thing he knew he was in the "house.""

"Man, I could steal the socks off a cop while he was directing traffic. I say I'm the best and you're afraid to put it to the test. " Lee glared at Mark.

Mark was silent. He thought about it for a while, "Firstly, that's exactly what I mean. What are a pair of socks worth? Why would anyone want to steal a used pair of socks? Especially off a cop! That's the dumbass kind of thinking that gets you locked up."

"Don't weasel out. I say let's do something together. I wanna see what you got. Pick something hard, something different, and we'll steal it together. After you see me work, you'll see I'm the best." Lee would not let up.

"Alright. It has to be something neither of us has ever done before. Something completely different. Something that requires two men." Mark's resolve weakened.

What harm could come of it? Suddenly he was willing to violate one of his most important rules. He would take on a partner but just for this one job.

"You got something in mind?" Lee's eyes lit up.

He hoped Mark would pick a big target. A job with a lot of money involved. Lee had enough of breaking into homes and robbing booze from liquor stores. The biggest thing he had done so far was rob the local jewelry store. He had done that twice. Mark had imagination. He was a cut above and Lee longed to be like him.

"You did the jewelry store on 7th street twice now. If you go back again they'll catch you." Mark took a dig at Lee.

"You know I did those? How'd you know?" Lee was shocked. He thought he hadn't left a trace.

"Of course, those robberies had your name written all over them." Mark picked up the local newspaper and turned to page two. "Look at this. This will be our target."

"I don't see anything, what are you talking about?" Lee looked at the page and saw nothing that looked like a target for a big-time burglary.

"It's right here, that's our test." Mark put his finger on a black and white photo of an old man in uniform feeding what looked like a large oversized house cat.

"That's it man, we'll steal that. Read the story, it's an Ocelot from South America, the zoo's latest acquisition. It has just gone on exhibit. I want it."

"Are you kidding? What in the hell would we do with an Ocelot?" Lee had hoped for a bank. At the very least some high priced jewels from a society matron. But an Ocelot? A zoo animal?

"I'd keep it as a pet. I'd be the only guy in the county with an Ocelot for a pet. Wouldn't that be cool ?" Mark looked slyly at Lee, would he do it? Would he go along with it?

"I thought we'd go after something worth a lot of money. Something heavily guarded. A challenge with a big pay off." Secretly Lee thought, a pet? You want me to help steal a fucking pet?

"You laid down the challenge. I picked the game. I say we bag the cat." Mark gave Lee a sneer insinuating cowardness was at the root of his reluctance.

"Alright man, but I'm losing respect. I figured our first job would be something big. Something special." Lee had dreams of hitting the big time. "I guess it's a start, sure, why not, a cat."

"I don't think it will be that easy. For sure it will be different." The idea of robbing the zoo had come to Mark in a flash of inspiration. It was a total departure from his routine.

"The zoo is surrounded by a fence. It is built to keep things in. I am sure it will be locked up in a barred cage. They probably have night security. So we will have to have a good plan. The thing we got going in our favor is they probably don't think much about people breaking in. The place is designed to keep the animals in. It is not built to keep people out."

The whole suggestion was a whim. Mark never thought Lee would actually agree to do it, but now that the whim was in play, he decided he really did want the cat. He looked at his expensive leather couch and thought how cool it would be to have a large beautiful Ocelot sitting on it, while looking out at the harbor. It would invoke envy.

Mark and Lee cruised the outer perimeter of the Oakland City Zoo. A fence ran parallel to the road and was the boundary marker for the entire western half of the zoo. Mark drove the length, and found the service entrance where food and supplies were delivered. Several uniformed zoo employees were unloading bales of hay. A ten foot high chain linked fence surrounded the grounds. It seemed very sturdy. They decided it could be cut with the right tool. There were a dozen or so cars in the parking lot. It was well lit and ringed by lights. It was too visible. It was not a safe or secluded entry point.

"We'll have to find a spot where we can cut the fence. We can't try to climb it." Lee spoke up. "We'll park the car where it won't get any attention."

"I saw a spot on the access road about a mile from the zoo. We'd have to walk a full mile. If we parked there." Mark offered.

"A mile's a long walk in. We need a spot close to the section where they keep the cat. Let's look for that." Lee suggested. "Once we get the cat in the bag, the real work starts. We need to get him out of the zoo and into the trunk as quickly as possible."

"You're right. Let's see where his cage is, and go from there."

As they walked through the entrance the ticket taker handed Mark a map.

"The Ocelot is new, they marked it in with an ink pen. It's right next to the monkeys." Mark showed Lee the map.

"That's bad. That's where they keep the big red assed baboons." Lee gave Mark a look, he knew the area.

"So?" Mark asked.

"Baboons are really loud when they are disturbed. If we wake them in the middle of the night they'll make a racket. There are dozens of them in that cage. It's a big outdoor area. You'll see." Lee was liking this less and less.

"His cage is close to the center of the zoo!" Mark pointed to the spot. "That means we will have to carry him at least a quarter of a mile to reach the fence."

"Yeah and it winds through a lot of exhibits. It is not a straight line.It will be dark. I'm sure they turn the lights out at night." Lee was now getting worried.

"It would be a mess if we got lost in here."

It was Mark's "challenge", he could not back out. He was also starting to feel uneasy about the whole thing.

It was Thursday and the park was not busy. They made their way to the Ocelot's cage.

A crowd had gathered to welcome the new star of the zoo. "Tommy", the ocelot was lying in the sun and stretching. His dappled coat was light brown, black, golden and white all at the same time. Mark thought he looked a little like a forty pound tiger with flashing yellow eyes. "Tommy" was indifferent to the zoo visitors.

'Mommy, he's just a big cat." A little boy in the crowd spoke up, disappointed and complained to his mom.

"He comes from South America and they are nasty, feisty animals. They're nothing at all like a house cat." Momma tried to make the cat seem dangerous.

Mark and Lee examined the cage closely. "Tommy" had a small outdoor door living space with a doorway in the back corner that led to a second cage where he slept at night.

"There's a locked gate leading to the inner sleeping compartment." Mark pointed to a chain and lock. "After we cut that lock we will have direct access to the inner compartment."

Overhead, a tram ride was circling fifty feet off the ground, giving guests a view of the zoo from the air. It passed right above the cage.

"Let's take the ride! We will be able to see the whole layout. It'll give us a great look."

Fifty feet to the left the baboons were wrestling and fighting out in the open air. A big male was asserting dominance and pounding on his chest. A light afternoon breeze floated their combined stink all over the grounds. The male was raising hell. His rage disturbed a howler monkey who began hyperventilating, taking in large gulps of air. Suddenly he started to scream until his voice filled the afternoon with cries of anguish.

"Tommy" leapt to his feet and started to pace.

Together the howlers and the baboons frightened the young boy who began to cry. He grabbed his momma's leg in fear.

"Let's take a look," Mark motioned to the overhead ride.

For fifty cents they were gliding freely over the cages and looking down into the Ocelot's den. It contained a sliding wooden door, with a chain and bolt that separated it from the entrance.

"After we cut the front lock it looks easy." Mark nodded confirming the plan.

"Yeah, right there, that's where we should cut the fence and get on the grounds." Lee was pointing to a spot marked by a towering Oak tree. From the air it looked like a clear and easy path from the fence to the cage.

"That's the closest point. It's the nearest spot in and out, and the path is pretty clear. We'll have to pass the monkey cages. That's our entry spot alright. We'll cut the outer fence right there." Lee spoke with assurance.

"We can park on the street and be in and out in twenty minutes or less."

"Yeah, but you saw what a racket those monkeys can make. If we wake them it will alert the guards for sure."

"You're right. We need to be quiet. No banging on drums or singing while we work." Mark smiled and winked.

The overhead tram passed above the elephants and the giraffes. Off to the left they were treated to a panoramic view of the San Francisco bay and the Bay Bridge that stretched from Oakland to the city.

"You know this place is kind of nice." The gliding ride made Lee feel good. "I should bring my kid brother here."

"I am really looking forward to owning that cat. It's gonna be nice to own something that's unique. Something that is one of a kind."

Mark and Lee traced and retraced the path from the Ocelot's cage to the big Oak tree next to the spot they were going to cut in the chain link fence. It was mostly clear sailing. A ten minute walk from the fence to the cage. The last one hundred yards was off the park pathway through the underbrush. It had some dense growth and high weeds. They tried to memorize the twists and turns of the exit route and Mark made some written notes.

"Twenty five minutes tops."Mark emphasized the timing. "That's how long it will take us to cut the fence, break in, and get to the cage and back out to the car. I figure ten minutes or less each way. plus five minutes to grab the cat."

"Piece of Cake." Lee could feel his confidence growing. This was going to work, but then he thought. "Why do I care? What's in this for me."

He didn't like the answer. Nothing. But then he thought about the idea of forming a future partnership and it would lead to bigger jobs and bigger money.

"You sure you want to share this beautiful place with that cat?" Lee looked around Mark's expensive apartment and shook his head.

Mark paid no attention; he was thumbing through the phone book searching for a listing. He found what he wanted and wrote down a number on a scratch pad, and dialed the phone.

"Hi, I want to talk to your employment department please." Mark waited and winked at Lee.

"Hello, yeah a friend of mine told me about a job in your security department. I am calling to see how to apply. I have many years of experience."

"Yeah, that's right, my friend told me you have an opening for a guard. I am wondering about the details."

"You don't have an opening on the night shift?" Mark responded by pretending he was surprised. " I was sure he said you were understaffed and looking to beef up. How big is the night time shift? Do you think you might have an opening any time soon?"

"Carl's the main guy and he's been there for a long time? Ten years. I see, does he have any backup? Could you use a backup? I have references." Mark gave Lee a bit of a look and signaled with his finger the number one.

"You might have a need for a back up? Great. When can I come in and apply?"

"I am interested, can you give me a few details on what the job would require. When does the night shift start work? "

"Nine pm to six in the morning. I guess you allow a break of about two or so? Is that right?"

"Sounds interesting. Thanks. I will drop by soon and put in an application." Mark hung up the phone.

"They have one night guard. Sounds like he's an old guy. Been there ten years and probably is bored to death. I'll bet he sits around and reads all night. I'll bet he naps half the time."

Mark picked up the phone and dialed the zoo switchboard again.

"Hello, I'd like to speak to Carl in security."

"He starts at nine? How can I reach him directly? Does he have a direct line? You're giving me security? Thanks, let me write that down."

He hung up and dialed again.

"Hello security. I am at the front gate and I'm having a problem. When can you get here?"

"Yeah this is the front ticket office. There's an unruly customer here and I need help with him. I think he may be drunk."

"Ten minutes? Okay hurry. I need help now. " He hung up the phone.

"The security office is located a long way from the front desk. From the sound of it, It's way in the back of the park."

"I think if we break in at two in the morning, he will be on his break eating his evening meal and will be far from the Ocelot cage. Even if he does hear us, it will take ten minutes or more to respond and we should be driving off by that time."

"That sounds good. How do you plan on taking the cat away?" Lee held up a large set of bolt cutters and snapped them together in the air. "These are damn sharp and will cut the fence and the lock."

"I bought a big burlap bag, we'll just throw it over him, and tie up the top."

"Tonight at two. I am going to get some rest." Lee felt comfortable, it would be an easy job.

The access road leading to the zoo was very, very dark at night. There were no street lights, Mark cruised along slowly looking for the big oak tree next to the fence. The tree had seemed huge during the day but now the trees were mostly hidden in the dark. Which one was the giant? They all seemed big and it was so dark he couldn't see the tops of them against the black sky. Which one was the really huge one? Mark stopped the car and looked out at the lights of the bay bridge. It was off to the right, just as it had been that afternoon. He turned the flashlight on the oak tree towering above him. It seemed huge but was it the right one?

"This is the one." Mark declared it was time to start.

"You sure? It's so dark." Lee's questioning voice was a little shaky.

"Yeah, pretty sure. But hell, once we're in we'll find our way around."

They parked the car and climbed up the small hill to the fence. Lee cut the links until he had made a six foot slit. They flipped it up and bent it a bit. It stayed bent and open, making it easy to enter the grounds.

"If we got this right, it's a hundred yards to the back wall of the children's petting zoo. We turn right there and it's two hundred yards down the path to the monkey cages."

They started walking through the brush. It was thick and there was no clear path to take. They had to fight and struggle with the underbrush. They were knee high in growth and each step seemed more difficult than the last. The underbrush was getting thicker, higher and more difficult to deal with. Mark shined the light off into the night and there was a building up ahead. It was fifty yards away and the brush was now three feet high and impossible to manage. They were cut off. It was a tangle of thick blackberry plants fully five feet high. They were being stabbed and scratched with every step.

"Is that the kid's zoo?" Lee's voice asked.

"I don't know, it could be." Mark shined the light over the field and looked for an easier way to approach. "We'll never get through this stuff."

"This doesn't seem right. It wasn't this thick this afternoon." Lee's pant legs had blood oozing out. He had been badly cut. "This is taking twice as long as it did during the day."

"You're right." Mark could feel the blood dripping down his own legs. "This isn't right. We need to change course."

Mark aimed the light over a patch of ground off to the right. "That looks easier. Move to the right. Fifty yards over. It is not so heavy over there. We can't pass here, it's just way too thick."

Lee followed the path of the light and things got easier. "You're right, it is a lot easier. Man, my legs have been cut up pretty good."

"Mine too. We didn't pick the best spot. But we're in." Mark answered. His legs were raw from battling the brush.

They reached the back side of the building, but was it the right one? It was pitch black out, and they had no idea where they were.

"We got to find a sign or something to verify where we are. We got to get around to the front and see what it says." Lee's voice was anxious.

"Yeah." They made their way around the back side of the building. When they reached the front nothing was lit, not the entrance ways, not the signs. It was all very dark. The beam of the light could only uncover a few feet at a time. Mark tried to run the light over the face of the building. He found a sign. "Insect and Snake exhibit." He tried to remember where that was located. But his mind was blank. He knew for sure they were in the wrong part of the park.

"Insects and Snakes. I don't remember seeing that." Lee was starting to panic.

"Calm down, calm down. I'll figure it out." Mark spread the map of the zoo out on the ground. It was windy, the map flapped in the air. "Hold it in place while I figure out exactly where we are." Mark frantically studied the map.

"Where are we?" Lee was very anxious.

"I'm still looking.It's hard to see in this light." He studied it for a long while. " Found it." Mark's finger jabbed at a spot on the map. "We're at least a full section over from where we want to be."

"Which way do we have to go?"

"I think we need to go left. That way." Mark nodded left.

"Are you sure?" Lee knew he was lost, was Mark sure?

"Well the bay bridge is on our right. I am using that as a starting point of reference. Given that, we need to go to the left. The alligator's are next, then a section with birds, then the children's zoo and then finally the monkeys. We picked the wrong place to enter."

"If you hear the guard's cart, just hide in the bushes and be quiet. He can't find you in the dark." Mark warned Lee.

Mark kept the light on the pathway, and made their way in the dark. The next sign said "Alligator Cages".

"We're on the right track now. It won't be long." Mark tried to reassure his young companion.

"Yeah, well we've already been here for thirty minutes. We were supposed to be in and out by now."

They found the kids zoo and a sign pointing to the baboon exhibit. They were on the right track. As they approached the baboon exhibit, they were relieved to find the animals were all inside the sheltered areas. It was still and quiet. They passed it in silence.

"There it is." Mark pointed to the entrance gate leading into the Ocelot's cage. Lee hurried over to the door that opened up the route to the inner cage door. He cut the bolts and the door swung open.

"Easy."

They entered and examined the lock to the inner cage. Inside they could hear the cat stirring. It knew they were out in the hall.

"After you cut the bolts, I am going in with the bag wide open. I'll throw it on him. You make sure he stays trapped in the cage until I get him in the bag. If I miss him, don't let him get loose. If he gets out into the open we're done. I'm gonna cut the bolt now! You be ready!"

Lee cut the bolt unlocking the chains to the inner chamber. Mark handed him the light.

"Shine the light in his eyes."

Mark charged in after the cat with the mouth of the burlap bag wide open. The Ocelot hissed and darted at him attempting to bite. Mark flinched. The cat retreated to a corner of the chamber. Mark advanced once again with the bag wide open. He lunged at the cat who dodged and scurried off.

"The bastard's really quick. Keep the light on him."

Mark dove at him again and got the bag partly on the cat's head. He put one arm around the body of the cat and tried to pull and shove him in the bag. It dug at him with its back legs. It ripped his shirt and continued to dig and claw frantically.

"Ouch! Shit he kicked me with his back legs." Mark let loose of the cat, it was partly in the bag but rolling wildly. It was tangled and frantic.

"Jam him in the bag." Mark yelled at Lee for help.

Lee dove into the fray. The Ocelot was kicking at the burlap with his back feet frantically tearing at everything in sight. Mark got hold of the lip of the bag and pulled it over the body of the cat while Lee jammed it's head downward. Mark cinched the bag closed and they dropped the bag on the ground. The cat was hissing and spitting and rolling around in the bag clawing wildly trying to free itself.

"We got him, let's go." Mark picked up the forty pound cat, who was getting louder and louder, while shaking with fury.

"He's got his claws stuck in the fibers and is ripping at them." Lee thought if he ripped hard enough he might even break the bag open and get loose.

"I think I know the correct way out from here. It's over that way. That's the way we scouted this afternoon. We came in at the wrong spot. Ouch, shit, he bit me through the sack." Mark's voice was loud with pain and anguish.

Just then the baboons woke up. They scurried out of the sleeping area en masse and gathered in a large group in the front yard of their cage. They all shrieked at the top of their lungs until baboon cries were echoing throughout the zoo. They slapped and pounded on each other in a frenzy, pointing at and complaining about the intruders, who were parading in front of their cage.

Mark and Lee hustled along, passing raging baboons, while their prized cat hissed and spit in an angry rage. It kept rolling and ripping at the burlap. Somewhere in the distance they hear a door slam shut and an engine starts up.

The howler monkeys suddenly began making a thunderous chorus of noise that only howlers can make. Their screams rolled out in bursts over and over again. With that, the lions awoke and started roaring. The entire zoo was awakened all at once.

They quickened their pace until there it was, the children's zoo and behind it the open field leading to the fence. Mark shined the light into the night. The light found and focused on the huge oak tree.

"We'll have to cut a new hole to get out and back on the street." They could hear the security cart sputter as it came down from the hills in the night. It was coming fast and headed straight for the monkey cages.

"Cut the fence open and let's get out of here." Mark dropped the heavy bag. The cat was still spitting and choking furiously. He was rolling around in the bag on the ground. Mark had to pick it up afraid that he might roll down the hill and out onto the street. The cat was so loud and making enough noise that anyone within a hundred yards would hear him. Lee cut an opening and they were out of the park and on the street.

"The car is a half mile or so up the road. Stay low and back from the road. I'll jog up and get it." Mark suggested that Lee stay with the cat.

"No way I'm not sitting here waiting with the cat making this racket. If the guard hears it, I'm screwed. We got to keep moving."

"Okay, grab an end of the bag and we'll run together." Ten minutes later they were driving off with their prize in the bag stuffed in the trunk.

"We did it." Mark offered a high five.

"Yeah, I guess we did." Lee slapped his hand.

They were both bleeding from a half dozen scratches and bite marks on their hands, arms and legs. Their hands stung badly when they clapped. They winced in pain.

It was four thirty in the morning when they arrived at Mark's parking lot.

"Help me get him up to my unit."

They carried the tattered burlap bag to the elevator. The elevator was resting on an upper floor. Lee pushed the button and they could hear the elevator start up. It arrived and the door opened. Mark did not know his neighbors, and had very little to do with any of them. But when the door opened, he recognized the owner of the unit just below him. He was a stockbroker and went to work early.

"Good morning." He looked at the two of them bleeding and torn. For a moment there was a look of shock in his eyes. "You're up early or out late." The cat hissed and tore at the bag.

"Yeah, good to see you." Mark averted eye contact. The cat had urinated while locked in the trunk, The bag was wet and smelled like cat piss. Mark's neighbor turned away repulsed by the smell.

"Geese, what you got in the bag?" He had his hand up to his mouth as if nauseated for a second.

Hearing the conversation the cat redoubled its efforts to escape. Mark and Lee hurried into the elevator and pushed the button to close the door.

"That wasn't good." Lee said.

"Yeah he goes to work early. I had forgotten about him. He has no idea what we're doing. I'm not worried. He'll forget seeing us."

They entered Mark's unit and dumped the burlap bag on the floor. They both sat down on the couch exhausted and stared at the bag with the angry roiling cat. A long silence ensued. Neither Mark nor Lee moved or said a word. A full five minutes passed.

"Well, are you going to let him out?" Lee asked.

Mark cut open the bag and jumped back. The cat struggled to get out. Finally it poked its head out and hissed angrily. It hesitated and looked at each of them as if sizing them up.

"Hiss." it dug its feet into the carpet and leaped forward racing straight at them on the couch.

Lee dived out the way. The cat bounced over the couch and vanished into the bedroom. Lee recovered and followed it.

"It's hiding under your bed. It won't come out. It's pissing under your bed."

The End.

Author's note: this story was inspired by a newspaper article in the Oakland Tribune in the 1970's. Someone broke into the zoo and stole an Ocelot. The following day the animal was found at the zoo entrance tied to the front door. It had been returned without an explanation.

Mack the Knife

Mack stood in front of the mirror admiring himself in his new velvet blazer. He brushed some imaginary lint off his shoulder, and looked again to see if this gesture had helped to obtain the effect he desired. He wanted to look stylish and elegant. What he saw was a young, unlined, boyish face grinning back at him foolishly. There was no sign of purpose in his face, he looked carefree and unharried. It was as if he had never endured a single hardship in his life.

Mack had a face that looked ten years younger than it was. This was both a blessing and a curse. It was a blessing, because the innocence he exuded served to excuse him from some tight spots. How do you punch a well meaning kid in the nose? There were times when people just shrugged and wrote him off, thinking someone that young and foolish could not be taken seriously. He was cursed because people never took him seriously. His near childlike demeanor had helped win an occasional friend, because as he had discovered, some people like a man who cannot be taken seriously.

It had also kept him from ever having a deep and meaningful relationship with anyone. None of any kind, not with either sex. Over time he became aware of this and knew that his was a strange, abnormal case. He was thirty years old and his voice had never changed. His voice was high pitched like that of a boy of twelve or less. He was a little under five feet tall, with one arm shorter than the other. A fact that perceptive people noticed when he tried to play pool, which he was not very good at. Somehow he always managed to scuff the cue ball, and send it on its errant way to doom. He was a master of the "scratch" shot, often sinking the eight ball prematurely. He played a lot of pool and almost always lost.

When he was in high school, he was ostracized and excluded from the groups he tried to be a part of. Eventually he left his small town and traveled. In his travels he searched for acceptance and as he grew older he found it. Nothing deep, nothing permanent, but he found comradery, along with a hardy laugh or two with a slap on the back now and then. He found it in bars, the temporary meeting places of people living in big cities where casual friendships were easily formed. But he also learned that these people drifted in and out, often going their separate ways. These "friendships" were fleeting and shallow. Mack longed for something more.

Mack was well known for buying drinks for others, sometimes he would even ring the bell and buy for the entire house. "Drinks are on Mack!" was a chorus that was often heard when he was present. That gave people the impression that he had money to burn, something that was never the case. Mack worked at a second rate job and lived as cheaply as possible, scrimping and doing without in many areas of his life. His daily sacrifices allowed him to be generous in the bar scene. Buying a round for a full house was a "show" he puts on.

His current hangout is a lively bar in downtown San Francisco. The Sutter Street Station at the end of Sutter and on the corner with Market. It is a place for all comers, no one is ever excluded, but no one is particularly included either. In this bar Mack had found a purpose. He was "in love" again. Mack fell in love easily but there was one problem. He had never had anyone "love" him back. Tales of unrequited love were his true theme song, playing and replaying his entire life.

Mack was a thirty-year old virgin. He spent a lot of time and effort trying to hide this fact. He gave frequent lectures designed to convince anyone who would listen that he was the reincarnation of Cyrano himself. He lay claim to being an ultimate authority about love, love making, and all things connected to love. He practised this speech, until he could deliver it with confidence, from beginning to end to anyone who would listen. In it, there was always a girl somewhere that he had left behind, or one that was waiting for him to return.

The woman "waiting" was always a luscious beauty who would vouch for his manliness. No one ever believed a word Mack said about his prowess with women. It didn't matter, no one cared. It was fun to listen and nod agreement and string him along. His high pitched squeaky voice made his story impossible to accept. Mack knew that no one believed him, but he carried on bravely, telling and retelling the same sorry tales. He often got the details of his stories mixed up and if anyone was listening for a second time, they knew it was crap.

"Mack, the knife, what's up?" John, an acquaintance, bellied up to the bar.

"Have you seen the new girl? Jay?" Mack's face lit up with delight at the sound of her name.

"Yeah, what about her?"

"Ain't she something?" Mack was aglow.

"I guess, I hadn't thought much about it." John finished his first double scotch by throwing it back with authority. He promptly ordered another one. "You like her?"

"Yeah, man she's fine. I'm going to get that one." Mack sputtered a little, glancing at Jay serving drinks at the other end of the bar. He had laid it on the line for the world to see. Mack the knife was on the hunt. The fair Jay was his intended conquest.

"Good luck with that." John gave him a brief sneer. John thought Jay was out of Mack's league.

The far end of the bar was filled with executives from Standard Oil. They were all tossing back drinks , laughing loudly, and carrying on. . The "Standard Oil" crowd was a group of "married men" who played at being high rollers. They were always looking for a good time. They played "liar's dice" and players came from all over town to get in their game. It was $50.00 a cup, and they played dozens of games a day. Big money changed hands.

They played for hours, often leaving late at night. They all covered up by telling their wives that they worked late every day. In truth everyone ducked out of the office by 3:30 every afternoon. They drank and played past 11:00 and always arrived home fully inebriated with excuses for the "little woman" about long hard hours, and excessive work requirements.

They all told the same story and backed each other up no matter what. It worked, they all showed up at the bar ready to play dice every day. Sane people believed that their wives saw right through their bull shit but didn't care.

These "executives" were all far too lazy to get up and go to the bar and order a drink. Every drink was hand delivered by a scantily clad waitress. Jay was their new favorite waitress.

They were big tippers, so they were her favorites too. She invested a lot of time hovering around them and chatting them up. For Mack they were the competition. He took a seat at their end of the bar. They ignored him completely. He started watching their game, studying them. They were the enemy.

"Hi!," he smiled at Jay,

"Another round for the guys: that is one scotch and water, two margaritas and two bloodies." Jay put in their drink orders.

"Only five this round?" the bartender asked.

"Yeah a couple of them are taking it easy, not ready yet." Jay answered.

"Can I buy you a drink Jay?" Mack asked, hoping to score points.

Get men to spend their money. That was Jay's job description in a nutshell. Never say no, just get them loosened up and spending money. It was part of the code. Pretty young cocktail waitresses were expected to accept free drinks from adoring men. Any and all men, no exceptions.

"Sure, I'll take a white wine, Chardonnay," she smiled at Mack. The bartender filled the order she had placed for the Standard boys. Jay motioned he should pour her a top end glass of wine.

Mack was thrilled, she had let him buy her a drink. How far would she let him go? Was this the beginning? His mind raced ahead, praying and hoping she would say yes to him. Once again, hope had sprung for Mack.

His imagination took off and painted a future life with Jay. He longed for the chance to make her happy. Part of him believed if she would say yes, it would be perfect. He would do anything to please her, all she had to do was ask.

The bartender placed the white wine Mack had bought her next to her tray. She picked it up and took a sip.

"Thanks, for the drink" her perfect lips formed a luscious round kiss which she blew at him. She winked and nodded and Mack went out of his mind with joy. Jay! Jay! All he could think about was Jay!

She was a beautiful girl, and she knew it. All her life men had bought her things, or offered to buy her things, and she always took what she wanted. She accepted gifts or tokens of affection without considering that there might be a string attached. She was oblivious to the concept of being in debt or of having an obligation to fulfill. Such an idea never once entered her mind. Good things just came to her. She figured she deserved it, and that is why she got things given to her.

Mack sat and drank by her station for hours. Every chance he got he offered to buy her a drink. She never refused. It got late. The Standard oil guys had all gotten very drunk. Captain Randy, a dice playing "executive" so named because of a stint spent flying a copter in Nam, had lost big. He was irritated.

The drunker they all got the louder they got. Randy was the loudest, and drunkest of them all tonight.

"I could use some luck," the Captain grabbed Jay and pulled her to the table. "Kiss my cup for luck." He rubbed her ass with his left hand and bent her head forward with his right one. Jay kissed his cup. He squeezed her butt.

He shook the cup violently in the air covering the opening with one hand and then he slammed it as hard as he could down on the table. The cup hit the table so hard that Mack thought he might have chipped the dice.

"Eight ducks. I say out of fourteen dice, eight are ducks." He started the round off by calling without looking at his dice.

It was a very high beginning call and Randy got some mean looks for pushing so hard, so quick.

"Out of fourteen dice, eight are deuces?" The next player paused. "You aren't giving me much room."

"You're calling to the big cup. He's clean. We gotta get him dirty now or he'll run away." Captain Randy's voice was edgy. He had not won a round all day. He made bad calls when he was drunk. His "luck" was not about to change.

" I call Nine Petaluma butt draggers.I believe I got a load of em." The next player, little Mike, accepted Randy's bluff and passed it along.

"Well that's nine deuces out of nine. Pretty tough to do, I call." Big Larry, the big cup, picked up. "I ain't got no ducks.No deuces. You missed my hand. You can't get there."

Larry had five dice and none of them were ducks.

"Crap." Mike pushed two. He glared at Randy. "You set me up.

"You didn't have to jump to nine, it's your own fault." Randy tried to make an excuse for his aggressive call.

"The Captain set you up, not me. That call was too high. Push two." Big Larry grinned, it was good to have all five dice, especially if they tried to jam your hand and missed.

"Shit, Jay, get your tight little ass over here I need a rub." Mike yelled across the bar at Jay. "I need some of your hot luck."

"You want me to kiss your cup?" Jay was at his side.

He put the dice cup up to her mouth for a kiss. Under the table he grabbed her crotch.

"Naw I need somethin hotter than that." he rubbed her pussy for a moment. She barely moved, pretending it didn't matter. He pulled up his hand and sniffed his fingers . He shook the cup violently. He sucked on his fingers, closed his grip on the cup and slammed the dice.

"Give me some Aces!" He peeked under the cup and smirked. "Luck is on my side."

"Four Aces, Killed them." Little Mike stuck out his jaw defiantly.

"You're pushin it." Big Larry peaked at his dice.

"Got to, I got the Aces, Jay gave 'em to me. I feel hot!"

Larry shook his head. He had all five dice; everyone else had two.

"It's going to take a lot of Aces to get there. I am going to pull it. I got one, you clowns have three more?"

"I got two thanks to Jay's hot pussy." Little Mike had two out of two.

This time they were there, four naturals. Big Larry pushed out two. The game was close again.

"Come here, Jay one more time for Big Larry Couley."

Larry was down to three dice, he wasn't feeling so big any more. He reached inside her pants and stroked her the opening between her legs several times. She squirmed and inadvertently looked at Mack.

"I got the juice boys! Let her rip! " He slammed his cup down. "Ten dice left, I call six fives."

Mack was a tiny man, all the Standard guys "dwarfed him." but he didn't hesitate for a second. He saw a call for help in Jay's eyes and he sprang up and rushed to her aid.

"Get your hands off her." His falsetto voice shook with

anger.

Stunned, the entire group paused for a second and then broke into laughter.

"Damn you," Mack squealed in his high pitched girlish voice. "Damn you all to hell!"

Mack charged out of his seat and headed straight for Big Larry. A wave of dizziness swarmed in his brain as he jumped up. He stumbled and tripped and ended up face first on the floor.

"You leave her alone. Get your hands off her." Mack struggled, windmilling with arms, while lying in a heap on the floor trying to get up.

"Or else what?" Big Larry mimicked Mack's high pitched tone. "Or else what?"

The Standard men broke into another chorus of mad laughter.

"I give you this boy, you got some balls." The Captain chimed in. "Especially for a little guy on the floor."

Mack got up and steadied himself. His mind cleared. When he felt able he lunged at Big Larry again. Once more he lost his balance and fell to the floor. Mack was very drunk.

"I'll get you. I'll get all of you." He yelled out from his spot on the ground.

"You gonna punch me in the leg?" Big Larry put his boot in the middle of Mack's back and pushed hard. "Get out of here. Bartender, this boy is causing trouble."

Mack was very shaking as he got to his feet. He was gathering himself for a final charge when the bartender's hands wrapped around his neck and the seat of his pants. The bartender picked him up and rushed him to the door and threw him out onto the streets.

"You've been eighty sixed. You are not welcome here again." The bartender's voice angrily yelled at Mack banning him from ever returning to the bar.

The trolley car went by in the late night and rang its bell. Mack lay there wondering what to do. The Boys from Standard were laughing loudly. Their happy voices filled the night. Mack could hear Big Larry and Captain Randy yelling at Jay to bring a fresh round of drinks. Mack imagined that Jay was at their table again taking their orders. She was and placed it with the bartender.

"I'm glad you did that." Jay thanked the bartender. "I was

afraid Mack might get hurt. He had no business getting involved."

"You okay?' The bartender asked.

"Yeah, I'm having a great night tip wise. One of the best ever." Jay went back to see if she could help in the dice game.

The Three Card Shuffle

It was after midnight in San Francisco, and I was alone, sitting quietly on the bus watching the stops fly past at breakneck speed. Normally I rode during the day, and all the stops were lined with passengers forcing the electric trolley bus to stop and start at each corner to take on passengers. Where were all the riders? I had never ridden this late at night before. The car was empty, the street was deserted. I was the only passenger, the corners were empty so the driver could bypass all the stops and was cruising down Mission street making excellent time.

I had been visiting a friend and had stayed later than planned. I needed to get to the transfer terminal by 1:00 to catch the last bus home to Berkeley. If I missed it I was stuck in the city for the night. It might be close but I felt a tinge of satisfaction as he rocked and weaved his way down Mission street. As each familiar street sign appeared and vanished from sight I felt relief. I was going to make it!

During the height of a busy day the same trip down Mission to the terminal took an hour or more. Tonight, I stretched my legs across the double seat, draped my arms leisurely over the back rests and let my head fall against the window. I was riding solo till he reached the transfer station.

Suddenly, without warning, the bus lurched to the right, shifting lanes like a skier skidding on powdered snow, sliding, until it came to a screeching halt. I bounced in the air, my head snapped forward at the suddenness of the stop. If I had been drifting into sleep, I was wide awake now.

A young black man, fashionably dressed in a suede overcoat, frilly white shirt, and baggy high cuffed pants, jumped on the bus the instant the doors swung open. He dropped a quarter in the meter, hurried down the aisle and thrust himself into the seat across from me. He glanced at me nervously and then peered furtively out onto the street. He stiffened in his seat as if a ramrod had been shoved up his butt.

He seemed terrified. His eyes bulged out and his lower lip quivered and shook. I thought he was going to shout at the bus driver. He seemed to be in a panic but he remained silent. A large man was running up from behind at breakneck speed, trying to catch the bus. I could hear him yelling for the driver to stop. Fear and panic lit up the eyes of the young man seated across from me.

The driver pulled over and waited for the sprinter to catch up. The driver opened the doors letting the large muscular black man onto the bus. I watched the newcomer closely, he was well over six feet tall, dressed in factory work clothes, his head was bald, having been shaved and that allowed the light to bounce off it. He thanked the driver for having pulled over. If you're not at the stop waiting they don't have to stop to let you catch up. It's the driver's choice. This time he had seen the big man running and stopped for him.

He was breathing hard, trying to catch his breath. He paid the fare and turned towards us. As he sauntered down the aisle a sneer formed on his lips and he glared at the man across from me. It was immediately apparent that they knew each other. The big man walked slowly forward, keeping his eyes riveted on the face of the other, hissing under his breath with what seemed like satisfaction.

It was as though he was a cobra holding his prey in suspended animation while he waited for the best moment to strike. He moved slowly, without caution, each step seemed to contain a growing threat of calculated menace. His walk, his look, and manner seemed impregnated with suggestions of measured violence about to be unleashed. He swung with an almost cat-like grace into the seat in front of the trembling young man.

"You ain't goin get away from me that easy," he drew his lips back over his teeth in a wicked smile.

"I ain't done nothin, you leave me alone." Mr. Well Dressed squirmed under the hard gaze and looked at me as if he was asking for my support. My quiet ride had been interrupted. I was no longer alone, I had company, one a slender fashion plate and the other an angry bear awakened from hibernation.

"You took my money and ran away, you gonna give it back now man." The bear's voice was surprisingly restrained but

I heard violence in his tone.

"Look here, I won that money from you fair. If you didn't want to lose you shouldn't have played." Mr, Well Dressed adjusted his coat and shot his chin forward with a look of defiance.

"You don't be playin the game if you can't lose. I don't make nobody play."

His voice cut at the larger man who winced at the suggestion that he did not have enough money to play. Well dressed shot me a knowing look, a look filled with patrician arrogance. His bluff had worked. I was expecting a fight, but now it seemed something else was in the wind.

"I don't mind losing, but I hate it when a man leaves when he is winning. You don't be leaving when you ahead if the other guy still want to play. You gonna give me back that money fair, like I lost it to you." The bear surprised me.

"You still got money man? I thought I got it all. Lemme see it, if you still got some. I don't believe you got any." He jerked his head forward with a little nod as if he were daring the bigger man.

"I got money man, don't you be thinkin I ain't got no money." The bear fumbled in his pockets for a moment and pulled out a ten dollar bill.

"See, I got money." suddenly he was eager, vindicated.

"Why didn't you say you weren't through? Hell man I can play all night if you still got the cash to lose," a broad grin spread across his face and he reached into his jacket and pulled out a small brown leather packet. The red queen of hearts flashed above the edge and caught my eye. He pulled out a ten dollar bill and carefully spread it out on the bus seat.

"Put yours down too or I won't lay down no cards.

The big man leaned over the seat, his shiny head sparkling in the bus lights. He placed his ten dollar bill on the seat. "You gonna lose that money back to me now."

"You see these three cards, one is red, the otha two is black. Just like before. You watch em close cause yo ain't never gonna find the red one." With that he began to shuffle them furiously until it was impossible to follow the red one. He clutched them all in his hand, guarding them carefully, and then in one quick motion laid all three of them out in a line. From where I was sitting I caught a little flash of red and knew that the winning card was in the middle.

The big black man hovered over the back of his seat like a

child intently caught up in a brand new game. He pondered the three cards for a long time letting his hand hover over each for an instant. Impulsively he chose the middle card and turned it over. He found the red winner.

"I toll you I was gonna win my money back," he gleefully snatched one of the tens, "Let the other ride."

"You just had a little streak of luck in a game of skill. I wouldn't let it go to my head." He shuffled again and again it was impossible to follow the flight of the red card as he shuffled and moved them around. Yet once again as he set them out in a line I caught a glimpse of the red card. It was on the far end. The big man's hand popped over the seat and pounced on the red card. He must have seen it too, I thought.

"You ain't so slick man," he grinned as he picked up another ten. He was winning and it looked easy.

"I jus lettin you win to make you feel good. I can afford to lose. You wanna play?" He turned to me and winked, flashing a big grin. He was inviting me to join the game.

Out of the corner of my eye I saw the lights and the entrance to the east bay bus terminal. I pulled the cord, it was my destination, the transfer station. I had a bus to catch and the schedule was tight. I walked reluctantly to the exit of the bus. I wanted to stay and play.

I had a nagging, almost irresistible urge to play, but decided I had to leave. It was late and I had a long trip ahead of me. An hour later I was in my bed in Berkeley sleeping peacefully and the entire incident was forgotten.

The incident would have remained forgotten, lost in the burial ground the mind keeps for the unplanned intrusions that life piles high on the average city dweller if chance hadn't stepped in. I was working in East Oakland at the time and was still using the bus services.

On this particular day, a Friday, I had a date with a girl in San Francisco, and when work was over, I headed out to meet her. I boarded the bus and found one of the few remaining seats. People kept crowding on the already full bus. Soon I was tightly wedged in against the window. The aisles were crowded standing passengers holding the overhead rails. I was glad I was seated. I had worked hard all day on my feet, and if luck was with me I would have the pleasure of a long night ahead of me. I began to read.

Just as the bus was rolling up the open bus lane and heading for the bay bridge, a hum of excited voices rose up in unison from the back of the bus. At first all I saw was a row of blank vacant faces all looking straight ahead. They all looked right by me without any connection being made. Then I saw the card player.

He was about seven rows back, sitting in the seats that face each other across the aisles. He was carrying on like the showman he was and had the attention of all those seated around him. He had a new and even fancier set of clothes. A gold watch chain was hanging from his vest pocket. He looked like a caricature of a Mississippi riverboat gambler. He was wearing a white Panama hat and kept smiling and throwing money on the floor. It didn't take long before he stirred up attention and was surrounded by a ring of people. They huddled so close they blocked my view until I couldn't see him anymore.

Every once in a while little bits of dialogue would filter through to me, I knew there was a lot of action going on back there. I tried to stand and get a better view of the situation but it didn't help. It was too crowded. I only made the people sitting next to me anxious. I gave up trying to watch.

The game noises, the sounds of winners and losers continued all the way to San Francisco. I fought off the urge to push my way back to watch. Finally we arrived at the terminal. It was a long half hour ride. The trip seemed like it took an eternity. The passengers disembarked and I hurried to the back trying to see the tail end of the game.

It was futile, the game had broken up as quickly as it had started and the card player had melted into the crowd. I felt disappointment, as I stepped off the bus. My curiosity had been aroused and I didn't want it to go unsatisfied. I noticed a person with a sour look getting off behind me. Had he been one of the ones in the game? He was almost the last to get off.

I turned to him, "Did you play in that game back there?"

He was about thirty with a baby face that was marred by what looked like a fighter's mouth. His lips had been battered and his nose was twisted and looked to be permanently swollen.

"Yeah," he answered and looked at the ground.

"How much did that guy win? The card player I mean?"

"Some, not much, He lost as much as he won. He'd win some and then lose some just as quick. He wasn't that good at it."

"Did you win any money from him?"

"Naw, I lost twenty dollars and my watch." He just kept looking off into space after each sentence. "Another guy lost more."

"Who won?"

"Some big dumb black guy with a bald head. He kept winning, I can't understand it though. He seemed so damn dumb."

I looked at him and shook my head. It all made perfect sense.

"Did it ever occur to you that they were partners?" I asked.

"No, they couldn't have been, They didn't even know each other."

He was looking straight at me now, a look of slow apprehension was breaking over his face.

"Well I've seen them work together before. It was a while ago. They almost took me in too. They definitely know each other well."

I headed off to the arms of my girlfriend. I guess I love to gamble, but not at cards.

The San Francisco Adventure

Night after night Councilman Griley lay in his bed unable to sleep. Griley was an important man. A man of influence in his hometown of Columbus. He was a well known pillar of respectability in his community and was committed to following the rules, and living up to the expectations of others. He was not yet truly old but he was closer to seventy than he was to forty. He had the terrible feeling that life was passing him by.

Lying in bed, he always found himself staring at the ceiling, while his wife slumbered next to him. Her snoring was a nightly problem that he had learned to live with. He no longer thought much about it. There were always intervals when she would stop breathing, they usually lasted several minutes making him think she might have died, but he had no such luck.

Inevitably she would react with a sudden jerk, her lungs would violently suck in huge gulps of air as they reacted to her oxygen starvation. Without waking, she would grab his arm, anchor herself in place and desperately gasp for breath. Her panic gulping noises were always followed by loud long snorting sounds that he found truly annoying. He imagined she was "A hog looking for truffles."

For a few brief seconds her eyes might open but they never focused on anything. Once her panic attack subsided she would find the rhythm of her breathing again and fall right back to sleep. She did this every few hours every night. They were so regular, Griley could almost tell time by the comings and goings of her attacks. When she woke in the morning she was without knowledge of any of it, and so had never once acknowledged them.

Her massive rotund body made the bed sag severely causing a slow suction that pulled Griley into her. She had made a permanent indent in the mattress, it had become a slippery slope. Griley fought against the pull but was inevitably drawn to her by gravity. The thought of contact with her made him nauseous and he fought desperately to avoid it.

To combat this he lay spread eagle every night trying to maintain traction and thereby saving himself the anguish of sinking into her. The rising mound of her belly held the sheets up above them both like a tent in the summer, when the air was hot and still, he felt some gratitude for this small blessing. In the winter it was the opposite, it caused him to freeze, and then he cursed the fates that kept his wife riveted on her back in this perennial position.

Her preparation for bed always began precisely at ten each night and the routine had not varied for years.

Tonight had been no different than any other, and she began with her ritual of verbal incantations.

"I feel so pretty, Oh so pretty." Mrs. Griley sang to herself and worked step by step to maintain her "look", a look only she had ever really appreciated.

"Mirror, mirror on the wall" Griley mused beneath his breath, mocking her vanity with a silent curse.

She always paid verbal tribute to the shining goddess she saw beaming radiantly back at her, "Perfection!", she often said as she patted her cheeks. The accouterments used in her constant quest for physical beauty consisted of numerous creams, lotions and ointments that all promised to take twenty years off its users appearance. In reality they did nothing but drain Griley's bank account.

The crescendo, the inevitable crowning touch of each night's ceremony, came after hours of tying intricate knots in her hair, when she wrapped a shawl around her head and bundled it in such a way that not a hair could be disturbed as she slept. Griley was not allowed to touch the masterpiece she was certain she had achieved. Her hair and her entire package was strictly off limits to him.

Her prohibition against loving contact was fine with Griley. He had not wanted any for a long time, he could not remember when it was otherwise. It was a reciprocal agreement. Creating the chance for an atmosphere of intimacy between them was definitely not the purpose of his wife's obsessive devotion to the shrine of beauty.

Defensively, he lay next to her heavily plastered form with real foreboding. Griley had developed his own set of rituals which took wing when hers ended. Each night as she slept, he lay quietly next to her in what was nearly a state of suspended animation. Without trying hard he found his mind rearranging and remoulding the surface of her face. In place of the deeply lined road map of antiquity she possessed, he imagined the features of a beautiful young man. A young man with the finely chiseled features reminiscent of a Greek god. An Adonis!

No such young man existed in Griley's circle of acquaintances but he had managed to piece together an image of perfection. Griley was greatly assisted by the use of an illicit magazine called "San Francisco Nights." When left alone Griley spent many long hours pouring over the pictures of beautiful half dressed young men in suggestive positions.

He had come into possession of several additions of
this forbidden magazine and kept them under lock and key
in his workshop drawer. They were buried hidden under a
pile of reader's digest issues that had never been touched.
The ultimate effect of his intense longing was that he was
now able to call up and project the likeness of his longing
for true love onto his wife's face..

At first, this transformation of his wife's features
had been casual, and without much success. The object of
his desire would appear for a brief moment and then vanish
into the shadows as quickly as he made it appear. In time,
with practise, the visions gained in clarity and duration,
until the Councilman could languish in comfort and lust in
the nearness of the warm intimacy of his creation. Now he
could summon forth the image of his young companion
with ease, and it became a common practise to do so; it was
an addiction that he found himself feeding at every available
moment. He felt he was Merlin reborn and living in
Columbus.

The pleasure of this transformation became more
acute with each imaginary unfolding. The Councilman
knew that his lustful imagination had awakened urges that
previously had been of a hidden and unknown nature.
Urges that he had always denied and up until this time had

not even acknowledged. His conjuring was instinctive, and without deep thought.

On this particular night he found himself on fire, burning with a desire to do it. To really do it! He knew that he had to have completion and the lure of the immense satisfaction it would give him called to him. He imagined the young man's luscious face, calling to him, urging him onward, until overwhelmed, he imagined the bliss of their ultimate union and cried out,

"By God, I'm going to do it!"

Gingerly he lifted himself above his wife's body, seeing only the boy's beckoning face. The boy's mouth opened and formed a circle. It beckoned! He inched himself slowly into place, he was old and it was hard to hold himself in the plane position. His arms began to weaken and shake. It was all he could do to keep from collapsing and plunging into him/her prematurely.

He found himself savouring the courage he had discovered, he felt a sense of joy as blood flowed into his extremities. It was as though he had found a reservoir of energy that was invigorating him with the ramrod vitality of youth. His penis was partially erect, it was the hardest it had been in years.

He hung there suspended above his wifes tightly
wrapped head, imagining a hot young boy in her place. He
was on the verge of his finest sexual moment when suddenly
his wife's eyes popped open just as he was about to plunge
into her mouth in a classic jack-knife dive. The shock effect
of her piercing scream caused him to abort and avert
completion. Instead of the deep dive he had planned, he lay
floundering limp on top of her while she frantically pushed
him away with all her strength.

"You Beast! You Beast! Get the hell off me!" Griley was at a
complete loss for words and could only cower and whimper
in fear of his wives' loathing.

He had been robbed at the very moment of
promise, the moment when he was finally going to achieve
true satisfaction. Instead of the glorious union his mind had
manufactured he was faced with her choking face spitting
in disgust, her instant rejection, her violent and abusive
torrent of verbal disdain. It was enough to make any man
shrink to the size of a pygmy. He had shrunk, his penis was
flaccid. She would have none of it, none of his reckless
sexual abandon. She let her anger rain down on him, until
he crawled away and hid from her.

Rolling to the side of the bed and cowering beneath
the sheets he realised that he had reached the ultimate

psychological consequences of his imaginings and he faced the truth. He knew what he really wanted, what really called out to him. It was cathartic, it was finally clear, even to Griley, what sort of a life he longed to have and what he must do to obtain it.

The result of this alarming event was to send Griley's imagination plummeting down an erratic course. He became like a pinball. For a brief moment he imagined that he might never gain equilibrium again. He knew he had earned the look of terror and absolute horror that had appeared on her face as she rained hatred down on him. She had rejected him with every fiber of her being. The truth was that the feeling was mutual and had been for years.

He could not shake it, He longed for the innocent glow and beauty of the perfect young man whose face he had projected onto hers. Where was the Adonis hiding? He knew the vision existed only in his imagination but the seed was real. The magic being had to exist. If not in this small town, then for sure in the promised land, the magical city by the bay.

Each day that followed brought an ever growing clarity to Griley's ambitions. He prayed for and was quickly gaining the strength to throw off his chains and flee to the glories of San Francisco, the royal kingdom of delight he had found enshrined on every page of his tattered magazines.

The bell had rung and it was calling him home, home to Baghdad by the bay.

It was as if a decade of self deception had melted away the veils that had covered his eyes and he could no longer tolerate the mundane existence of his life. Mrs. Griley seemed not to notice the changes in him. They should have been evident but it hardly mattered, she had never really cared. He seized the earliest opportunity and fled to San Francisco. When he left, she pretended not to notice.

He was a man obsessed with a mission. The mission was to find and enjoy the physical embodiment of his ideal lover. He knew for certain that he was out there waiting for him. He was calling him, luring him onward, with his girlish and boyishly pretty face. He had long curly eyelashes. He was slender and feminine and yet was a grown man. He was young and innocent, and always smiling in his mind's eye. He beckoned Griley onward.

Griley arrived in San Francisco with his mind in a haze. He struggled, lost in foreign city, his path was being guided by lust. In this confused state he trudged the streets and alleys of North Beach anxiously searching, always believing that the next face would be the one. He grabbed strangers by the arm, twisting them around and thrusting himself up into their faces frantically hoping that the next apparition would be the physical embodiment of his own imaginings.

"What the hell, let loose of my arm". They always reacted in horror.

"Sorry, sorry, I thought I knew you, sorry."

Lust had laid him low and he vaguely realised that he was becoming a public nuisance. Then it happened!

Griley was awestruck, he stopped in his tracks, frozen where he stood. A young man, in light summer clothes, was standing at a bus stop waiting for a bus, he was gorgeous. It was crystal clear that without a doubt he was "the one". It was as though a providential protective hand had reached out and shook Griley's soul.

He was a young Tyrone Power with long flowing hair and the eyelashes Griley was fixated on. The boy was alone, available, and best of all no one else seemed to notice him. He was approachable. It was as if they all were blind to his beauty. Griley gathered himself up, certain that destiny and fate had led him to this moment. He approached the boy with confidence and certainty.

"Hi, how you doin?" he asked.

There was no response. The boy did not even look at him. There was no acknowledgement. As Griley got closer to the object of his desire, he saw that the resemblance to his imagined lover was exact. It served to reinforce his certainty that this was meant to be. It could not be an accident. He had found the "one".

"I am just visiting your town, I like it a lot, I'm alone, by myself, how about you?' Griley grabbed the boy's arm and drew him close.

"What are you doing, you creep." The Adonis pulled away angry.

"I been looking for you. I finally found you." Griley tried to put his arm around the boy.

"Found me? What are you talking about?" The boy tried to get away but Griley had a firm grip on his arm.

"I'm an important man where I come from, I'm a Councilman. You're pretty, you know that? You're pretty, I'll bet your mom and dad are pretty. Are you waiting for a bus?" Griley wrapped himself around the boy and rubbed up against him.

"What in the hell?" the boy's voice deepened, he became strong as he glared at the Councilman. The boy withdrew from contact and looked anxiously up the street for his bus. It was late and the bus was nowhere in sight.

"Come on, I have come a long way to find you. I have been lookin for you for days. Be nice now!" Griley cooed.

There was no response. The boy pushed hard and Griley let go of his arm.

"I'm an important man, I got a lot of money."

" You're drunk and crazy" The boy answered, and was right on both counts.

Griley lost patience, this was not how he had seen it, it was not supposed to be this difficult. The boy was meant to be his, nothing less would do.

"I want you to come with me to my room." Griley lunged out at the boy who sidestepped his rush and avoided him easily. "You belong with me." Griley fell to one knee and reached up weakly towards the stranger who owned his heart.

"You're full of crap." The boy shouted and then kicked Griley in the ribs.

The bus arrived and opened its doors. The boy bound up the stairs, and quickly vanished. Griley watched as the bus sped away down Columbus avenue and into the night taking his prize away as quickly as he had appeared.

Griley's heart dropped into his stomach.

"You son of a bitch!" he screamed, but it was useless. The bus carrying his dream turned around a corner and vanished from sight.

Stunned, Griley retreated to a nearby bar, how could this have happened? He had been sure of his vision and the boy was an exact reflection of what he had seen in his mind's eye, so how could it be wrong? He had known the boy would appear but he had not expected rejection. He started trying to drown his sorrows in alcohol. He tossed down a second and then a third.

"Hi!" a husky voice cut in over his fantasy and woke him from his stupor. It was a large husky woman with indistinguishable features. She slid into the seat next to him and leaned towards him. She leered at him with one eyebrow cocked over her drink.

"How are you?" She had on heavy makeup and a red wig. Her lips were large and rosey, but her lipstick was smeared. She slid her hand under the bar onto his leg and stroked the inside of his thigh. She grabbed his muscle tightly and Griley marvelled at how strong she was.

"Hi!" Griley was barely able to respond. He blinked out at her, unable to focus clearly.

"I'm Liz," she said in a voice that seemed to be getting deeper as time passed.

"Is that short for Elizabeth?" Griley tried to make some small talk, his mind was still reeling from the disappointment of the lost boy.

"Lizard," the voice responded.

"How's that?" Griley looked at the figure again.

"Liz is short for Lizard, but the Lizard is not short."

The person seemed to swell and grow in stature. Griley became aware that he was seated next to a very large person.

"Let me buy you one." Liz signalled the bartender who responded quickly. "You look like you could use a friend." Liz rubbed the inside of Griley's leg again, this time creating more friction while lightly brushing his member.

Griley tossed down the drink Liz had provided and bought a round himself. Griley wanted to unburden himself. He wanted to erase the pain, the ache he felt. Liz seemed to be offering him an easy avenue, a place where he did not have to work very hard to find attention.

"I came here lookin for someone." Griley was amazed that he wanted to share this information with another human being.

"We're all looking for someone." Liz shot back,"If you don't find them, you have to keep trying."

"But I found him, at least I thought I did. He was exactly as I had pictured him. He was on that corner over there across the street." Griley nodded out to the street.

"Really, when was this?"

"Just a moment ago, right before I came in here." Griley was feeling the disappointment swelling up again. "I can't believe it happened."

"That you found him?" Liz was stumped at what to say.

"It was over so quickly. It is as if I had imagined the entire thing. But I know it was real. Why else would I be here?"

Liz bought another round of drinks and then another. Griley began to lose track of where he was and why he was there. He found himself strangely attracted to the resonance in Liz's voice; there was something in the way her tones moved up and down in octave levels that he found fascinating. She rubbed his ass and Griley knew he should have been offended but he wasn't.

Griley told her the story of the young man, and how he had come seeking him, and how he had found him on the corner, alone. Of how he had been left high and dry as if the whole pursuit had been a mistake. As he told the story it grew less painful.

Liz seemed to understand, he was not crazy and imagining things. A bond of comradeship formed, Liz had all the answers, Liz was there to rescue him. Soon Griley found himself staggering through the damp San Francisco night to Liz's apartment.

She thrust him onto her bed and vanished into the bathroom. "It will only be a minute." Liz reassured him that all would be well. Griley saw her reflected in a mirror on the wall, she was wiping away the make up from her face. "Just a minute more my love," The voice was deep and bear like now. "I am coming for you, my love." Liz was right next to him now and was pulling off the councilman's undergarments. The red wig was gone and in its place Griley was confronted with a balding head breathing hard and a hairy body heaving against him hard forcing open the cavity in his buttocks and splitting him in two.

Griley passed out and in his mind's eye he saw the young man again grinning at him as if he were teasing him. Throughout the night Griley was awakened by hot and cold flashes and by the persistence of Liz who seemed to find him wonderful. Liz was huge, much bigger than imagined and far more powerful than Griley. Griley was unable to resist or to respond beyond allowing the lizard to have its way. As the night passed Griley grew to accept his fate.

Morning came, and Griley awoke in pain. His whole body ached in places it never had before. He was instantly aware that it was icy cold. The window was wide open and the lone sheet that covered them was fluttering above him. It was perched tent like on the extended belly of the omnipresent Liz. Liz was snoring loudly, Griley ran his hand over the hairy stomach and pulled himself close for warmth. It seemed as though he were being sucked into the crevice formed in the bed by their combined weight. They slid down in it together. He drew closer for warmth and wondered what summer nights were like in San Francisco. Liz's beard had grown more prominent, she needed a shave.

The Short Unhappy Life of Terrence McAkers

McAkers stood in front of the bathroom mirror combing his razor cut into a perfect duck's ass. On this day Terry was paying particular attention to the long side sweeps of well oiled hair that trailed down to form a flip at the back of his head. Once he was sure that was stylishly in place, he could refocus on the little tuft of hair that hung over his forehead. His steely blue eyes followed the motion of his hand with a practiced precision that had developed through years of training and care. The image he cultivated, and rigidly adhered to, was as much dependent on the neat arrangement of his hair as it was on the black leather jacket and motorcycle boots he always wore. His life without them would be meaningless, and he knew it.

Throughout high school he had worn them like a badge of honor. They shielded him from being ordinary. Now, two years later, he could recognize how important they had always been. He was a "bad" dude. He had always been a "bad" dude and his hair and his clothes screamed that out to the world. They were a warning, "don't mess with me." He could still see the looks of fear in the timid eyes that were afraid to stare too long, but couldn't keep

from looking at him as he walked into a room. He
commanded attention.

He took real pleasure in being a badass and he made
that clear to all. He could still feel their eyes on the back of
his neck as he passed them in crowded corridors, the
pleasant memory of his "domination" filled him with joy. It
made him jerk his chin up, and look at himself with
satisfaction, as he slid his comb into his breast pocket. Most
girls averted their eyes, and wanted to get far away from
him, but the ones who counted,looked him straight in the
eyes with a resolve that told him what he wanted to know.
He was their kind of guy.

He had purposely avoided graduating high school.
Badasses don't walk down the graduation aisle, that was for
chumps. He had cut plenty of classes, gotten in numerous
fights and had even attacked a teacher. It was the assault on
the teacher that had finally gotten him permanently
expelled, and allowed him the freedom he had longed for.
The history teacher had pushed him a little too hard and
Terry had thrown a right cross to his jaw. The fat balding
old man had fallen hard like a bag of potatoes. With that
one punch high school was over for good.

Terry found and opened a small plastic bottle he used to store whites and reds. He took out two little white tablets and swallowed them. "Bennies," he thought, the breakfast of champions. The thought made him chuckle, "I'll be up to speed in an hour." he said out loud. He put a supply for later in his pocket. The floor of his little room was littered with beer cans. He picked up a partly full bottle of Jack Daniels, and shook it. He drained the little bit that was still left from the night before. The "taste"made him thirsty for more.

Today was a day like so many others, he had nothing to do. McAkers did not plan things, he just let them happen. He decided to go for a ride. He gave into an impulse to take a long ride, a ride to anywhere, it didn't matter. He strapped his black saddle bags on the back of his Harley and began filling them. He soon had them bulging with a rolled army blanket, a canteen filled with water, an army mess kit, and some dirty eating utensils.

"Have to get some supplies." he said to himself.

He stopped for a second and stared coldly at a battered oak chest that lay in the corner of the garage. His eyes narrowed to slits as though he were making a crucial decision. He nodded to himself in approval and opened the heavy oak lid. The cold steel barrel of the sawed off shotgun felt good in his hands, he put it and a box of cartridges in the second bag. As an afterthought he tossed in a couple of shirts, a pair of pants, a can of chili, and some beef jerky. He tied down the bags and was ready to go.

      The garage door responded with a thud, when he pushed it open a bit too hard, and stepped out into the early afternoon sunshine. The good thing about sleeping to noon was you got to skip the morning. He lit a cigarette and leaned back against the side of the tiny shed, mulling over where he wanted to go. Nothing came to mind, nothing. He would just get going and when he got there, he would be there. It would be enough to ride in the wind.

"One place as good as the next." He reassured himself that not having a plan was as good as anything.

    A loud roar filled the garage when he kicked the starter pedal down hard. His body tingled with a manly sensuality as he straddled the bike, pushed it forward and gunned it onto the street leaving the door open behind him. The warm air felt good against his face as he wove through the back streets of town towards the main drag. The streets were dead, they were empty except for a few children playing on the sidewalks. They did not look up as he passed, he took the bike up to fifty.

Without thinking about it, he cruised by the local hamburger stand racing the engine as he passed. No one was there. No one even looked up. As he passed the pool hall parking lot he saw it was empty except for a couple of old station wagons. He didn't know the owners. No one of importance was shooting pool today. "Nothin' is goin on today". He cruised by without stopping and pulled into the entrance of the local shopping center.

He idled up to the liquor store, parked and went in with a full swagger, making sure that all were aware he was in the store. As soon as she saw him, the old lady behind the counter fetched a pint of Jack Daniels, and put it on the counter. It was his usual order. He combed his hair again, looking at himself in the mirror behind the sales counter. It was amazing how much damage the wind could do in just a few seconds. His one dangling curl was out of place.

"Are you old enough to buy this?" It was a game she played with him.

"Yeah, you've checked me before, how many times are we going to do this?" he asked, taking his wallet from his back pocket. He opened the wallet and flashed her his fake I.D.

"Two dollars eighty nine cents " she rasped out. He paid with a five and gave her a dirty look.

He took his change, slipped the bottle inside his coat pocket," I just figured someday you'll remember me since you ask every time."

She shrugged and looked back at him annoyed. "I always check everybody. It's the law."

He had obtained the goods once again. He decided to cruise by the local movie theater. Standing at the entrance, dressed in a sports coat, with a white shirt and tie was a guy he had known in High School. The guy was talking on the telephone and looking at a pretty blond chick who was selling tickets. McAkers paused for a moment, parked and then approached them.

"What's up chump, you working here now?" McAkers took the sports coated straight dufus by surprise.

"Yeah, that's right," the "dufus" smiled as he recognized the source. "I haven't seen you since high school, what are you up to?"

"You mean since I got thrown out of high school."

"Yeah, I guess that's what I mean." The dufus nodded remembering the famous right cross.

McAkers ignored the question and spoke to the girl, "You know this guy you work with is a pacifist? Real fool, he doesn't know what a jungle this world is."
The girl didn't answer and just stared at McAkers.

"I know exactly what the world is like Terry. It is violent like you say. But that has nothing to do with my ideas about how we should act in the world and don't bother her while she is working."

"You're a blind fool in my eyes, and always will be. You must answer a knife with a knife. That is the way it is and that is the way it will always be" Terry spit out his argument.

"McAkers, you'll never get it. You're as stubborn as the day I met you." The "dufus" shrugged, turned away and went about his business. "If you're coming in, buy a ticket, otherwise we are working here."

McAkers seethed inside, "See you around chump.

You're dumber than rocks."

Terry was angry, somehow he couldn't intimidate that guy. He had no respect. Why would anyone think like that guy thought. What did he see when he looked out at the world?

It frustrated McAkers. He pulled onto the freeway and headed south.He had fifty bucks in his pocket, and an idea flashed in his brain, It said "Time for some fun!" He took the bike up to seventy five and cruised, he wanted to go faster. The road was clear in front, he took it up to eighty five. The bike hummed and became a part of him, it was steady, even at the higher speed, it made him feel powerful.

The beach appeared on the right and ran along next to the highway. He could see the waves rise and curl, and fall. He reached into his pocket and carefully broke the seal on the pint, he bit the cap and twisted it open and took a swig. It burned as it went down. For a moment he let the bike steer itself, and drank and then replaced the cap. The bottle was half gone.

The urge in his groin told him where he wanted to go. Old Mexico. The bike surged forward, and the road to Tijuana lay open before him. He worked the bottle. It went down smoothly and he was feeling fine as he neared the border crossing. Just as he approached the customs stop point, he finished the bottle of Jack. He threw the empty bottle over his shoulder. to the side of the road. It bounced as it shattered into little pieces. A road sign blurred past, he was just able to read, "Border One mile, Get Insurance at Haynes Insurance."

McAkers chuckled at the tourists who bought insurance every time they crossed the border for a couple of days. "Suckers and chumps," he said out loud.

He slowed, the freeway road turned into multiple lanes leading up to guard booths. Each had a customs officer waiting to ask the appropriate questions. Where are you going? What are you planning on doing? McAkers thought for once I should tell them the truth, tell them what I am planning on doing.

"Hey, I'm goin drink a lot booze and find a woman to fuck."

His mind flashed to past episodes of sex with dark eyed senoritas and whiskey and codeine in cough syrup bottles. Maybe I should tell them that I am going to get stoned and laid.

"I'm goin drink a bottle of cough syrup, smoke some weed, chug a lot of whiskey and find a woman to fuck." He said it out loud and laughed. What would they do?

No, I will tell them I am going to see the Jai Alai match. They will buy that, they always do.

The traffic in front of him opened briefly. He angled the bike and deftly cut into line at the last moment. The driver behind him honked, braking hard to avoid a collision, McAkers glared back and the man looked away frightened. He avoided eye contact and any possibility of a confrontation.

Suddenly the Mexican customs officer blew his whistle and waved him forward without inspection. There were no questions asked. He entered into old Mexico.

The streets of Tijuana are mostly paved, but many back ones are dirt or gravel. McAkers wanted to revisit a bar that lay a bit off the main drag and was soon sliding around dirt corners trying to locate it. The last time he had come here, he had gotten nearly everything he was looking in one place. He hoped to find the same crowd of drunken willing senoritas once again.

He soon stopped at a cantina that looked vaguely familiar. There were two young plump women standing out in front, smoking. They looked to have some promise, and one said "Holla" as he parked and dismounted.

Inside, on a raised platform, a woman was topless, dancing in a g-string, about three feet above the clay floor. He took a seat and ordered a bottle of tequila, his buzz was wearing off. He started downing shots, watching her large full breasts swing and twirl. She was grinding her hips to the sound of latin music playing on a scratchy old phonograph. A quarter of the way through the bottle, the booze began to take effect. McAkers put both elbows on the platform, rested his chin in his hands, and lurched forward with his hungry eyes bulging up at her.

She dropped to her knees in front of him, and pulled down the g-strap to her knees. She exposed a dark hairy shaved bush, that glistened in the bar light. He tried to pull her from the stage attempting to lick her but she resisted. She slapped his face and laughed at him. A chorus of laughter came from all parts of the bar and filled the room. Terry felt humiliated.

"You drunk loco gringo." She kicked him in the head.

Terry took the blow and tried to reach out and grab her.

She danced off the stage, leaving him alone at the front of the bar facing a room full of loud threatening men. They all continued to whistle and make sucking and kissing noises.

"Kiss this gingo." the voices rang down on Terrence.

His face reddened with anger, he grabbed the bottle and headed for the door. He staggered as he backed out the swinging doors.

"Fuck off, all of you." He screamed in the night air.

Chorus after chorus of hoots, howls, and whistles coupled with wild laughter answered back. Bottle in hand, angry and humiliated, he backed out onto the street. The swinging doors clipped him in the rear as he left.

The street was dark, lit only by the lights of the bar. He bumped into a small roundish woman who had been leaning against the wall blending into the darkness. She threw her arms around his neck planting a wet hot kiss on his lips. He kissed back harder, and put his hand on her ass, "You come with me." She pushed even harder back,

" Si! I come".

He pulled her along with him towards his bike. She came willingly, and put her hand out to feel his crotch and squeezed his member. It was limp and he was angry.

"Time for that later."

In the dark night he saw a small figure bent over the saddlebags on his bike trying to open them. The figure was pulling and tugging on them.

"What are you doing asshole?"

It was a shadowy figure, hard to see, he turned in fear, Terry saw his eyes flash in the moonlight.

The figure tried to run but there wasn't room to maneuver, he was trapped. McAkers was on him in a second. Terry brought the bottle down hard on the dark face and the glass flew apart with a loud cracking noise. At that moment McAkers realized his nemesis was only a young boy. The bottle had left a deep gash on the boy's cheek. His blood was spurting out, and landing on the face and blouse of the woman Terry was dragging.

The boy dropped to the ground with barely a sound, blood was flowing freely from the gash, McAkers stood above him briefly shaking in anger. He pulled the woman up to the side of his bike,

"Get on".

She looked back in terror, "No, not want to come, no".

He slapped her hard across the face. She stopped resisting, and climbed up on the seat. The bike fired immediately and he fishtailed down the street as men began to come in numbers out the bar in pursuit of McAkers. In terror she called out to them to help her.

 He could hear them screaming and yelling at him. He paid no attention. He leaned the bike into a corner turn, dragging his boot in the dirt as he went. The woman clung tightly afraid of falling, whimpering in Spanish. He growled at her to shut up and took another corner at high speed. He yelled over his shoulder, "Sex, si, sex?" "Fuck? Fuck?".

    She didn't answer. Her face and lips were drawn into a frightened pout. Suddenly she looked very young to him, much younger than he had imagined. Her face was almost childlike. Oh well he thought, I am in Mexico and anything goes here.

    A siren sounded in the distance, and then another much closer. He imagined that they were for him. He had to get off the streets. He slid into a side street and came to a halt. There was a small motel with a neon sign. There was a vacancy.

He pulled in, she tried to slip off the back of the bike. He pulled on her hand, not letting her go. She fell to the ground and lay there crying. He unhooked the bags, threw them over his shoulder and jerked her to her feet. She resisted, he tightened his grip on her arm, and pulled her to the front of the motel.

The door swung open easily at the touch of his shoulder. A thin scraggly old man rose from behind a wooden desk and approached with a limp.

" A room signor?" he had a high nasal whine.

"Si pronto".

The old man cackled as he took a key from the peg board that hung on the wall.

 "Si Signor, pronto." He pointed down a narrow corridor and held out the key, "Ten Pesos."

 McAkers shoved a couple of dollars in the old man's hands and pushed the girl down the hall. The old man grinned a toothless smile and shook his head,

"Si Pronto."

He let out a high shrill laugh that echoed down the hallway. Abruptly a door slammed and the sound of a latch clicking into place.

"Si, Pronto." The old man laughed loudly and lustfully again.

McAkers locked the door, the room was about ten feet wide with a sink and toilet in one corner, there was a surplus army cot barely four feet wide jammed against the opposite wall. The room was dimly lit. There was a single chair against the wall between the cot and the toilet, above it was a window to the street. The window was covered by a badly stained sheet. It served as a curtain. Outside the motel sign blinked on and off alternately lighting up the room and then letting it go dark.

McAkers threw the saddle bags across the seat of the toilet and turned towards her, "Take your clothes off."

"Si signor," she whimpered, "Si." She fumbled with her blouse, ripping off a button that fell on the dirty tile floor.

She had a bulging ring of fat on her stomach and was darker than he thought.

"You're not much to look at."

The sound of sirens rang down the alleyway, the police had found him. She had undressed and was now naked on the cot. She suddenly lunged forward, dropping to her knees she wrapped her arms around his legs,

"Si signor, we do it"

He felt very drunk, all the booze had caught up with him. His vision was blurry. She reached for his belt and tried to undo it. Her hand found his zipper and she pulled it down. "Si signor, we do."

She tugged frantically at his pants, crying and laughing,

"Si Signor, fuck fuck"

"Stop it damn you!" He was limp and flaccid. He pushed her away and onto the cot. She lay there crying, and sobbing.

There was a knock at the door, "Signor, the police are everywhere. Are they here for you?" It was the old man's cracked voice.

"How the fuck should I know. You dumb son of a bitch."

"I suck you, get you hard." The girl was on her knees pawing at his groin.

"Put your damn clothes back on." He yelled at her. McAkers went for the saddlebag and pulled out the shotgun. She was wailing and crying in a continuous stream piercing his ears.

"Damn Bitch, shut the fuck up." She continued to scream. She wouldn't shut up.

Terry fumbled with the gun. She had her arms around his knees and was trying to kiss his crotch.

"Stop it damn it, you dumb...stop it.."

She was relentlessly grabbing and squeezing. She pulled on his arm and hand. His gun went off splattering her back with buckshot. The blast left blood red chunks stuck on the wall.

A policeman's shoulder bashed against the door which started to break! The bolt latch flew apart and the door splintered as the latch gave in. The door opened wide.

The Federales with guns drawn entered the room. McAkers put his lips around the barrel of his shotgun, and closed his eyes. His tears were wet upon his face.

"Nothing to do today." He said and pulled the trigger.

Yesteryears Snows; A Novella
" In the Beginning There Was A Harmonica"

Jeff hunches forward, he is hiding in the narrow entrance of an old sea cave. His arms are wrapped around his legs, his chin rests on his knees. He imagines that the sea is breathing, slowly in and out like a dreamer mildly restless on a sheet of sand. He imagines the moon the night before has something to do with it all, he ponders the connection. It had hung like an off-white smile turned on its side. All night he had stared at it, feeling sure that it was vibrating at a slower pace than usual. He thinks, "All things vibrate, I can feel it.".

The entrance to the cave is crammed between two steep canyon walls that rise on either side. They seem to fix the beach in place. Gusts of wind frost the tips of the waves as they roll into the circular opening the lagoon has made. He jerks his head nervously at the sound of feet scurrying over the sand. No one is there, the beach is empty. What did he hear? It is mysterious, surely something was there, where is it hiding? Where did it go? The grey overcast morning seems threatening, he tries to relax, knowing that soon the gloom and the cold will burn away and the world will welcome the heat of the midday sun.

He begins to breathe slowly, imitating the rhythm of the waves as they turn over and out before him. He makes himself one with the momentary hollow curling in the wave as it hangs in the air. He becomes the "hollow". The water closes in on both sides,and he feels himself diminishing in space and size, he becomes the wave as it rushes to the shore. He is grinding crystals of sand in his teeth, sucking them out to sea and leaving behind the dead remains of an empty shell.

The shell is the crown of a lost kingdom. A voice calls from within. "I alone have the time to count the number of shells left behind and know how many grains of sand have been savored on the tip of my many tongues in the shaping of eons." Jeff falls forward prone in the sand and lies still. A voice full of denial rises in protest, it hovers over him, it cries out with pain, it begs for mercy. He blocks out these strange thoughts.They are dangerous. He thinks, "was that the voice of God?"

A hand takes hold of the nape of his neck and yanks on a scruff of blond hair. Liz lifts his sleeping face from the sand. His eyelids open and his eyes roll back so that only the whites can be seen looking skyward. The protruding eyes frighten her, it seems as if they might roll out of his head. She lays him sideways in her lap and brushes the sand from his lips. She begins to sing in a low husky voice that rises quickly to a lilting soprano. Her words are to an unknown song, one she is creating in that moment. They rush forward and hover above the sound of the sea.

Liz decides to wake him gently, romantically. A seagull makes shrill noises as it skims across the water. She bends over and kisses him. He stirs and awkwardly brushes her hair from his face. He opens his eyes and smiles up into her full moon face hanging colorless above him. She presses her lips on his, they slide off. There is no strength in his lips to press back. He turns his head and rubs his nose against her belly. He tries to lapse back into sleep. She won't let him doze off again.

The sand beneath her buttocks has begun to feel very hard, she shifts trying to get it to mold around her mounds. It is cold and the wind is cold. It bites through the thin dress she is wearing. It makes her nipples stand up and point outward. They are at attention but no one notices or cares.

She shakes him, pushing her breasts forward so that he will see them if he opens his eyes. A look of disappointment sets on her face when he does not see the hard ready nipples. He was supposed to wake up charged with energy, his every cell lit by the force of her song, and then seeing her aroused, became so himself. Instead he is quiet, almost comatose, motionless in her lap, and she is uncomfortable. Hunger begins to gnaw at the bottom of her stomach, it is enough to make her squirm.

"Wake up," her voice is curt. He turns on his side and stretches one arm around her waist. A low satisfied groan escapes from between his lips. It annoys her.

"Wake up!" Let's go to the Cottage for breakfast." Liz shakes him vigorously.

He rolls off her and pulls himself into a sitting position. His eyes are blurred and she looks foggy, the edges around her are soft and liquid. A little knowing smile forms at the corners of his mouth. He almost remembers. The cave seems smaller, more contained with her in it. It now seems small and womb-like. He wants to tell her that they are in the belly of mother earth.

"The tide is coming in, it will soon be up to the mouth of the cave and we'll get wet. Let's go." She does not want to sound impatient but she tugs on him hard, and tries to get him moving. He lifts himself to his feet, wavering with uncertainty.

"I burn up my energy so fast. I'm like a furnace inside."

"I know, you have such a strange mind." Liz puts her arm around him and helps him across the sand. He is feeble, the sand between his toes seems heavy, he can barely lift his feet.

"How did you know I was in the cave?" They climb a wooden staircase that was built precariously into the side of the cliff. It is old and needs repair, the steps sag under their combined weight.

"I woke up and you were gone. I just came looking for you, I found you right away, I don't know why I came to the cave but that is where you often are."

He feels that they are attached by an invisible bond that has always existed. He imagines that he drew her in with an invisible cord, can't she see it too? For a moment he wants to explain it to her, tell her about the stream that flows between them but it is too slippery, much too elusive for words.

Halfway up the staircase they pass a bearded man with a trench coat wrapped around his body tightly. Jeff ponders the connection between them all.

"Let's go back to the apartment and get Mike, and then go and get breakfast." They reach the top of the stairs, and Jeff turns in time to see the bearded man vanish in the opening of the cave.

"He must have wanted something, but he was just a bit too late. He missed his chance."

"Who?" she asks.

He knows that Liz saw him enter the cave, how could she act so stupid? It's a game, they don't want me to know, the two of them are in it together, I'll play along.

"He's gone now anyway," he looks at her harshly. She smiles back.

"When did you get up this morning? I didn't hear you leave." She likes that he is moody, she never knows what he will do next, he is never boring.

"Just before dawn. You were still asleep and I felt like taking a walk."

He is still suspicious of the man who had gone straight for the cave. What was he up to? What did he want? Did Liz know him? He had looked at her and his eyes had lit up. He was sure she had seen that. Had she looked back?

The top of the stairs opens on an alleyway lined on each side by a wooden fence. Two silver garbage cans stand next to a gate in an alluring way. He feels an urge to explore, to find out what is inside of them, but no, she is here. He feels restricted, cramped; she does that to him, it is like she always wants to control him. She has placed the cans off limits.

He notices a face frosting up a window right above the fence line, he sees two eyes watching them closely. She seems not to notice the eyes in the window. Instead she pulls him hard trying to get him to walk faster. He stares up definitely into the eyes in the window, the curtain falls, and swings back and forth. The eyes vanish.

He makes his body limp and refuses to lift his feet. He has formed a plan to explore the cans. She puts both arms around him and squeezes, afraid he is about to fall. He lurches into her, pinning her against the fence. She strokes his hair, she likes when he is aggressive like this. She hugs him to her breasts letting her hair wrap him like a cloak. He searches the window again but the eyes are gone. She must have sent them away. There are never any eyes watching when she doesn't want to be watched. He marvels at how clever she can be.

"How do you do it?," he whispers in her ear.

"Now, now," she is grateful when he responds to her. "Don't ask foolish questions, love." She feels mysterious, and it makes her happy.

He remembers the garbage cans and is overwhelmed by the need to spill one. As carefully as a man balancing on a tightrope, he shifts his weight and falls violently against a loaded can knocking it over. He mumbles in an embarrassed tone shifting his eyes shyly from her face to the mess at his feet and back to her face. He pretends to apologize, hoping to catch her off guard, and then gleefully begins to shift through the debris. He pretends to put it back in the can, while he takes it out and examines it piece by piece. Some of the trash makes it back into the can but most of it slips through his fingers and piles up on the driveway. He sorts it, hoping to find some nugget of value, but he finds nothing but garbage. It hardly matters, it is a momentary triumph. He has beaten her. Caught her off guard and gained control of their life together.

Somewhere inside Liz may suspect him, but he feels he has managed to arrange the act with such precision that she does not know it was deliberate. He has perfected the art of imitating a clumsy oaf. If she does suspect him, there is nothing she can do about it, so he basks in his own personal glory. He celebrates his fall as an act of power so subtle only he can truly appreciate it. He scoops up a handful of wet coffee grounds and flings it back into the can. Some of it sticks on his fingers, he wipes it on his pants. He looks into her face and sees that she is disturbed. She finds his actions disgusting, his hands are filthy. He is now covered in wet coffee grounds.

"Please, please, leave it alone. I'm sorry that I knocked you over." Liz apologizes. He has convinced her that she is the one to blame. She panics and tries to rescue him from the situation. For the first time she notices the face in the window watching them.

"Someone is watching us, let's go." A shrivelling up feeling grabs hold of her and she feels she is in the spotlight. The eyes in the window have become intense. She feels their disgust and it makes her skin crawl and she wants to run. Her instinct is to hide now that she knows they have been detected.

A wave of anger boils up in him at the idea of running. He thinks why? From whom? Where? It must have been a trick. He is certain that she has conjured all this up in order to mold him to fit her tastes. He pushes her away and sees the eyes again himself. They are there in response to her inner needs, they are there at her command, she always has some useful tool outside herself she can conjure up in a moment of crisis. Something she can use to put pressure on him to obey. Suddenly the whole thing is too convenient, it has the appearance of a master plan. She has conjured the whole affair up to counter his spilled garbage can victory.

In desperation he gathers up a wad of saliva from the back of his throat and coaxes it up into his mouth until it spills out and runs down his chin. That will throw her off for a second, he thinks. She never knows how to handle a stream of spit dripping from his face. He refuses to move until he has finished his treasure hunt. He quickly begins to rummage through the remaining garbage, opening bags of wilted produce and rotten egg shells. The look on her face tells him that she is becoming desperate. He knows he is winning once again. She cannot stand what he is doing. He rejoices in how easily he has turned the tables on her.

"Jeffrey, I cannot stand here like this another second." She grabs him by the collar of his coat and tries to lift him off the pile. Her voice is fragile and wavering, still she tries to regain her lost command. The eyes in the window have strung a line directly into her soul. They hold her responsible for what he is doing, they judge her with him as if they were one and not two beings. She knows it is all her fault, he fell because of her. If she had been more careful, none of this would have happened.

Obstinately he rips open a shopping bag while pretending to place it back in the can. To his surprise a rusty old mouth harp that someone judged to be junk is miraculously saved from doom. A spontaneous look of sheer joy and delight spreads across his face as he turns the harp in his hand, examining it as if it were the key to a complex puzzle he has been trying to solve. He holds it up to the sky and peers through the reeds to see if they are clogged.

"Looks okay. I can see the sky."

He slaps it against his thigh to dislodge any tidbit of waste or coffee grounds that might be hiding. He wipes the playing surface on his shirt. Cupping it in his hands he blows a string of notes until he reaches C. He closes his eyes and inhales the note making it quiver with a bluesy moan. The alley way seems to become alive with the dancing melody he has called forth. The notes seem to enter his lungs and fill them with vibrations that bound and rebound back and forth between the walls of his chest. It is as if the sounds are in tune with his inner essence, he becomes delirious as he exhales a long sustained note that pierces the quiet early morning air.

Blood rushes to her cheeks and she flushes a bright crimson. She wants to cover her ears and hide her face. She can no longer look to see if the eyes in the window are still present. They must be, but she cannot face them, the shame is too great. Instead her arms go limp and they dangle at her side.

His playing gets louder with more dissonance, it thunders, it screeches, it seems to mock her. She senses the irritation of people shaken from sleep, she knows that they are turning half awake in their beds. In horror, she ponders how violently the music the violence has inflicted on the neighborhood. She knows that the town is furious, and she is to blame. She waits submissively for the chorus of voices to rebuke her. But only silence ensues.

A sea of faces opens below him. They sway in unison, they've come to dance. He taps his foot and shakes his body trying to draw the rhythm up from his guts. He knows that this is his time to shine. He wants to take his new fans with him, and rock them into bliss, and carry them into the clouds. Then when the moment is right, he will let them down gently and return them to the earthly plane.

He envisions letting them float down, with him in command, until they are all resting on a pillow of air suspended above the stage. He bends over the harp and bobs his torso in time to a tune he hears in his mind. He sees his own face looking back in the mirror, his hair is wild and tangled, his eyelids droop and sag. His mouth hangs passively down as if it can no longer resist the force of gravity. His skin is pale white and his cheeks sink beneath the bones. He is skeleton thin and lays against the fence exhausted for a moment.

But the fans, his fans are with him, he has them in the palm of his hand. They energize him. They're on their feet, clapping and dancing. Their voices come howling back from all corners of the auditorium each time he blows a crescendo. It is magical, he wants to reach out and caress them, commune with them. He draws them into the center of his being like a magnet pulling filings across a blank sheet. They are there, he feels them all, swelling inside, filling his being. He blows out one last note slowly exhaling and holding it, draining every ounce of pleasure he can from it until his mind goes black. Then the crowd vanishes.

He turns in a whirl and rests his hips against the fence again, throwing his head back against the wood so that his hair hangs down freely and his face looks skyward. Grey clouds move slowly overhead. Seagulls caw, he imagines that it is the last bit of adoration that his fans can offer him. He nods his head in humble acceptance. The harp dangles silently at his side.

The sudden quiet seems almost violent to her. It is suddenly so still it frightens her. She is drained, defenseless, robbed of her vitality. She has no idea what to do. He has cut off from her, left her stranded. He has erected a barrier that she cannot cross. She wants him to grab her, to rush her to safety but he stands mute and indifferent. The eyes in the window have vanished and will never show themselves again. She waits for outrage, for anger to come bursting forth but the voices are never raised.

Instead he leans against the fence, lethargic and silent. Instead of the expected inevitable outrage, the neighborhood is silent and they are ignored, it is as if they do not exist. No hands are raised to quell their trespass, she freezes inside. We are alley cats, the disgraceful thought flashes through her mind. Despicable!

He focuses his attention on her; she is framed in the lines of buildings, patches of color, the shapes of shrubs and trees, the length of the alley way itself, all seem to fall into perspective around her. He feels them tug at him with a sly unity, a unity that she gives meaning to, is it because they revolve around her? It must be so, he decides. He puts the harp in his pocket and faces her.

"What's the matter?" His tone is casual, hiding his hostility.

Liz cannot bear to answer him, doesn't he know how he has exposed her? His voice has disarmed her with its innocence. She relaxes. Maybe he is right in acting as he does, there seems to be no harm done, no one really cares. The world does not revolve around their actions, she understands that no one really sees or attaches very much importance to them.

"Did you see the eyes in the window? Looking at us?" she asks, knowing he saw them. Why doesn't he care? She stamps her foot.

He thinks that together, they are no more than a brief sensation erupting and disappearing between yawns, hardly more noteworthy than two cats yowling on a fence. She buries and hides her insecurity from him. She locks it up in a secret corner of her mind and tries to forget the key. As she smiles her face becomes an invitation. She hopes it will reopen the door between them. He has been so cold and distant. That will never do. Her warmth turns to coyness, she makes her body shimmy slightly and steps toward him with slow little steps she thinks are dainty.

"What were you doing?" Her voice is sultry, she tries to fill it with wonder and respect. "It seemed like you were in another world while you were playing."

"I have always wanted to play the mouth harp," He says with a swagger.

Mission accomplished, he is feeling manly. He draws himself erect and allows her to wrap around him. Her admiration and eagerness pleased him. He smiles condescendingly like a benevolent God who is aware that he has sacrificed his divinity to be with a mortal. He believes that she has caught a glimpse of his true being, of his elevation. He decides nothing needs to be said, the moment speaks for itself, he lets it seeth as part of the understanding between them. She caresses and strokes his face lovingly. He forgives her.

Encouraged, she takes control, confident that she has at last reached him. He warms to her advances. They kiss long and hard. He runs his hand across her back and down over the firm hard lumps that are her buttocks. She shivers and giggles, he laughs sensually. Momentarily unconcerned she forgets about the spying eyes and clings to him more tightly rubbing against him with her thighs.

The friction sets his body rushing towards her. He pushes back, caught in the tidal pulsation of her rotating hips. He is drawn into her each time the contact recedes. They rock each other, she feels good, desirable; an unfathomable mixture of woman and child. She has his blood racing, his mind centered on her and her alone. She whispers in his ear. He nods and lifts her skirt while she fumbles with the zipper that always seems to get stuck at the wrong time. He enters her, they unite, she wants him, she is wet and ready for the divine union. She stands on her toes like a ballerina rising up to fit herself on his exposed erect member. All thoughts of the world leave them as they climax quietly in the alley.

Flaming Angels

The little room is clouded with smoke, the stereo reverberates. Jeff is drawing with intensity on a sheet of paper tacked to a cork board. His hand moves with a quick sureness. He is sketching an emerging vision that is issuing forth from the recesses of his unconscious mind. It is a picture of flowers and clouds. A candle flickers in the middle of the room, its glow casts a circle that spirals up to the ceiling. Mike lies on his back and watches the light. Suddenly, Jeff jerks to his feet, scrambles to turn off the stereo and blows out the candle.

"What's the matter?" Mike is startled.

"Is the door locked?" Jeff looks frightened and crawls towards the door on his hands and knees. He is trying to stay below the window line. He does not want to be seen.

"Yes, Why?"

"Are they both locked? Are you sure?"

"Yes, what are you doing?" Mike is mystified.

"I don't want him here. Not now, I couldn't handle having him here right now." Jeff's voice is frantic.

"Handle who? Who are you talking about?"

"He came up to me on the street last week. I brought him here. He's coming back. " Jeff's face is a ghastly white. There are footsteps coming up the walkway, Mike realises someone is approaching.

"Maybe, if we stay out of sight and don't make any noise he'll just go away." Jeff's head rotates as if it is on a swivel being pulled by a string. "He's coming up the drive and he's not alone." The steps have arrived at the door. They are hovering outside and for a moment the quiet stillness of the night is all that Mike hears or feels. "I think he knows we are here."Jeff's voice is quiet, like a whisper.

"Who is he?" Mike does not see the danger.

"Flash. His name is Flash."

A loud knock at the door cuts off the conversation. Mike can see Jeff's face in the moonlight. His eyes are wide with fright. The knock comes again only harder, it rattles the screen door shaking it on its hinges. To Jeff, it is as if an invisible hand has entered the room and announced with determination: "I will enter".

"He knows we are here." Jeff is paralyzed unable to move.

Wood scrapes on wood as the window is forced open, it is followed by the rush of an ocean breeze swooping in like a body climbing through a window, then the curtains blow back, and the moonlight is hidden behind the shadow of the intruder. Flash has broken in.

"Click" and the inside latch has been moved from its holding place. Heavy boots knock over rotting steps and the kitchen light is flicked on. Flash with his hair curling in knots beneath his shoulder smiles at them with a toothless grin. Jeff thinks of a shipwreck lying on the ocean's bottom peaking above the waves carelessly rusting away. In his hands Flash has a mangy alley cat with green eyes that seem to sparkle with anger. The cat hisses and claws him. Cut and bleeding, Flash drops the cat on the floor.

"I thought you were here, I want you to meet Ed," as Flash says, a large man with a purple flowing robe and a full beard enters carrying an open bible.

"The brother has informed me that you are one with the capacity to grasp and accept my message. I have come to inform you of the arrival of the inner cosmic reality." Ed's voice booms with authority and fills the silence of the room.

The alley cat hops sideways as if it has been struck by a bolt of electricity. Its claws scratch against the wood floor as it tries to get traction.It spins and slips, unable to maintain a straight course. Jeff thinks it cannot walk, only hop sideways. It has likely been drugged repeatedly.

Jeff decides the cat may be blind on its left side as it crashes out of control into their only chair. Stunned, the cat escapes the clutches of the chair and plows headlong into a bookcase. It begins to do frantic battle with the bookcase. The force of the collision causes a heavy hard bound book to fall out. It digs into the cat's back. The cat reels in pain and frantically begins a merciless defense, clawing and tearing at the attacking villain. The book is torn and slightly shredded and lies defeated on the floor.

"The people did not turn to him who smote them
nor did they seek the Lord of hosts,
So did the Lord cut off Israel's head and tail."

Ed's voice is a loud baritone and it seems to bounce off the
walls having an echo-like effect.

Flash dives to catch the cat but misses. The cat frantically
climbs the walls as it circles the room. Flash gets one hand
on it, but the cat squirms loose and claws him, drawing
blood once again. Angry, Flash refuses to give up, and dives
on it, trying to smother it, Under his breath he mutters
obscenities about the need for obedience. The cat squirms
loose, causing Flash to lunge once again. The cat hides
under the bed out of reach. It hisses and spits at Flash.

"In the desert the chosen
are gathering again
to heed the words
of the host of light."

Ed pauses, he closes his bible. He wants the full significance
of his message to take effect on his audience. Flash gives up
on the cat letting it hide in safety. He turns the stereo back
on, turning the volume up as high as it will go. He touches
his toes and stretches out his arms leaning backwards as if he
is preparing for an athletic event. He screams out a loud
"Ha" and kicks his leg in the air into an imagined foe. The

cat cowers under the bed. Jeff fidgets nervously. Mike sits dumbfounded on the edge of his bed.

"In the desert where the night air is clear and unclouded by the static of the city there are energy centers where the will of the powers that be are caught and recorded by those with the right sensitivities." Ed is talking to them whether they are listening or not. He pretends to be unaware of Flash dancing and the cat cowering.

Flash kicks his legs more vigorously, making vicious attacking motions. He balances momentarily next to Mike, he seems threateningly close, his arms slash wildly through the air. His hand cuts past Mike's face, missing him by a fraction of an inch. Then he swings straight at Mike's nose with the full force of his body behind the blow seemingly bent on cracking Mike in the face. His hand stops dangerously close to impact. He grunts, changes direction, lets his body dip and jumps backward, throwing a kick that swooshes by Jeff's unsuspecting head.

"I hear the words of the great prophets predicting the ability of a "free" mind to grasp the infinite. All they could really do was mark the road by showing the process. I on the other hand am engulfed in the process and expect to become one with infinite reality. I expect to master the process of grasping all that happens in each moment of time as it exists. There is a great flood coming that will drown our civilization. I have been commissioned to show those who can follow the path how to avoid this destruction and gain true liberation."

As Ed's words rumble to a close, Flash spins in place and kicks the wall with the sole of his foot knocking a hole in the plasterboard, one of Jeff's paintings of the sea comes loose and falls to the floor. Flash and Ed clasp his hands together in unison and bow smiling at Jeff and Mike, the two disciples they have chosen.

"You must come to my retreat in the mountains. There I will initiate you both." ---
----

The Call

It is late afternoon and the rolling hills of Mexico vibrate with a mixture of reds, oranges and light browns. An occasional strip of dying green adds variety as the car glides along the road. A powder white outline of a cow's skeleton picked clean flashes by, and Jeff thinks of visits to the graveyard to honor fallen ancestors whom he has never known.

He remembers flowers left to the nearly forgotten who are honored without real memory or mourning. Clouds of dust rise up in spirals that swarm across the bones polishing them as bits of sand making them gleam and reflect the light. The wind is strong and it rocks the car as it jostles over the potted highway towards San Miguel. In the distance, shadows cast a line into a hillside seeming to form a dark wedge on the side of the land.

"When the wind drives straight into the hills, it slices them open," Jeff's voice is muffled in the whir of the engine. Jeff imagines a mighty hand forging the land, compressing eons into moments, he hears the ringing of steel against steel as if he is in the presence of a blacksmith hammering endlessly away. For a moment, the hills seem to part, as if being cut by a knife, they become separate from the will of time. He understands all is truly unity, the moment is exquisite.

"Even the dust is dancing in time to the ringing of the hammer. I can feel it, everything makes sense."

"What makes sense?" Mike hears him.

"Everything is synchronized, it is all moving in a perfect pattern." He responds to Mike giving him a deep penetrating look which says, listen to me, I know.

"It will be night before we get there. The sun is going down."

It is the fifth of May, a celebration lies ahead. The beach is sure to be packed to capacity with Americans seeking an excuse to go mad momentarily. The road winds and twists causing Mike to slow down. Jeff's anticipation mounts, and time seems to become unbearably slow. The last rays of the sun sink beneath the water line as the road bends and opens onto a beach dotted with a thousand tents. Bonfires are already raging, the air seems thick with electricity. Jeff stiffens in his seat, as a rocket streaks the sky, and then explodes prematurely. It sends an umbrella of light and sparks dripping down on the people below.

"That one was defective." Mike notes as people react in anger at the carelessness. There is a toll barricade directly ahead but the arm is up and the office is closed. The beach is open for the weekend, free of charge. Mike pulls into an empty space and parks.

"Remember where I have parked. If we get separated we can come back here to meet." Mike knows that Jeff has a tendency to wander off and get lost, and warns him to stay close..

"I don't want to have to leave without you. Make damn sure you are here on Monday morning if you get separated from me."

"Let's see what is here." Jeff stares out the window into the confusion manifesting all around him.

He opens the door to the sweet smell of pot. It is the first thing he notices. The smoke is so thick it seems to hang like a haze covering and obscuring the people who are cluttered in bunches. Each group plays its own music as loudly as possible so that the sounds conflict and sound like they are dueling for dominance. Each gathering carries on independently, but to Jeff they create the illusion that they are one people, united in a cause of some kind. He wants to feel brotherhood, fraternity at its best. He is hopeful that the weekend will bring something like this thought to fruition.

It soon becomes apparent to Mike that most of them do not really know each other. He takes the lead, carefully avoiding the fallen body of a "comrade" passed out and blocking the walkway. Not far away a huge tent has been erected in a corner of the hamlet, it attracts Mike's attention.

"Let's see what that's about." Mike nods towards the tent.

They cut and squeeze their way to the entrance. The tent is jammed to capacity. To Jeff everything seems to be slowing down and each person seems to mock him. He is not sure why but they seem to all be mimics making fun of him. They mean no harm, but he feels that they see what a fraud he is, how shallow he is, and how much he does not belong. Jeff's head starts to bob from side to side and he focuses suddenly on a man in the distance sitting at the center of the tent.

He has a forest green field of light surrounding his body and the light and his body are rocking in time with Jeff's own myoptic motion. For a moment they seem like the only ones in the tent as they rock back and forth together. The whole tent has a texture of forest green but then the wavelength vanishes and Jeff can no longer pick the person out of the crowd. Who was he?

"The person lying next to you has not moved for several hours." a voice calls Jeff back into time. There is a body prostrate lying face down in the sand a foot from him. "I am not sure what he took but he might be dead."

Jeff is annoyed at being brought back into the moment so harshly.

"He's probably locked into his own thing." Jeff does not want to get involved.

"I thought he might be a friend of yours, that's all," Jeff sees the voice belongs to a stocky clean shaven mature man in his forties. "I want someone to take him out of my tent, Christ I can't stand burnouts."

Jeff decides to leave, the idea of dragging the body out of the tent overwhelms him. He doesn't want to do it.

"I don't want to be involved, I can't do it."

He suddenly realises that he has lost Mike. He leaves the tent to search for Mike. At that moment a man with his mind lit up like a roman candle swoops past howling in a mad dash to the sea, his voice is loud and filled with pain. With his arms extended he dives into the ocean plunging into the sea. No one reacts, it is as if it did not happen. Jeff looks to see if the man surfaces but the water stays smooth and there is no sign of the diver.

"Strange, he should surface."

He waits expecting the man to break the water line gasping for air but it never happens.

"Strange." He says.

Jeff stumbles forward and becomes aware of two lovers locked together in the fury of orgasm, they do not notice him.

Jeff's mind's eye is lit with a momentary image of two faces, one male, one female, superimposed on each other. He realizes he has fallen into their love net, somehow he has become part of their intercommunion brought on by the intimacy of drugs and sex. He feels their heat, mentally he indulges in the idea of wetness brought on by orgasm, "Have they invited me into their net?"

As soon as he asks the question the image changes. The man is seen standing on two rocks with an open ocean flowing between his legs. He is the Colossus imagining himself to be the heir to an ancient Greek god. The woman is sailing on wings through a cloud, she is alive with love she generously offers to mankind.

"They hardly know each other." Even though they have been tockingin a love embrace, Jeff realises they might even be strangers.

The intensity, the intimacy seems to ebb away, it dies, and their passion dies, leaving them two heaving bodies breathing hard in the night air. They become cold and uninteresting.

"Mike" Jeff calls out at the top of his lungs. There is no answer. Jeff finds himself climbing a winding dirt road with only the light of the moon and the stars to guide him. Three figures in white robes climb before him, they seem to beckon him onward, there is a hint of some deep necessity to follow. They are shadowy, like wisps of air. The urge to follow is strong but Jeff is still uncertain,

"Who are they?"

They vanish for a moment but each time when the road turns they reappear. They seem to be calling him forward, as if to a destiny he has always expected and is now awaiting him at the end of the road. He feels something Holy in their presence that frightens him, he wants to run away, to turn his back and flee.

They lead him further into the hills. For a moment he sees them clearly, the mists seem to crystalize, they are majestic with full flowing white beards, light shines, emanating from their faces. The vision fills his being and he begins to run to them,

"Faster, run faster" he bounds furiously up the hill "Must catch them, find out for sure of who they are."

He is almost certain they are the "Three wise men" but he must hear it from their lips. They are straight ahead glowing in the night like beacons, he is right on top of them; they are waiting, they have their arms stretched skyward in adulation, lungs bursting, he throws himself at their feet and grabs at the hems of their robes.

Vapor and mist are all he grasps as they slip through his fingers in the wet heavy night air. No one was there, he was following a mist. He buries his face in the sand and cries. He feels his tears become one with the ground. Too weak to move any further he lies there sobbing, understanding that he is alone. He feels he has always been alone.

He raises his head, half in fear, half in hope. He finds he has been lying prone in front of a neatly stacked pile of logs. "How did they get here?" It occurs to him that they must have been put there by someone and he is thankful that someone has piled up a windshield in the middle of the Mexican desert.

"Am I being hidden? Protected?"

The mist and the night are enough to keep him from view. For an instant he feels fear, fear of appearing ridiculous, how could he explain any of what he has just done if someone asked?

"Why should I have to explain!?" his voice breaks the silence with a screech. " I could pour ashes in my hair and go naked if I wanted to." this time his voice is closer to a whisper.

He lifts himself to his knees, the wood in the pile begins to move, it is a very slight movement but he knows that somehow the wood is moving. The cut planks take on new shapes, each log seems to become a miniature human body, they move in unison, overlap and entwine.

They seem to become a pyramidal progression stretching backwards and forwards in time. They offer an endless stream of caressing and beckoning hands outstretched in a curious waving motion. They are calling him. The hands are calling him!

He fights the urge to fling himself among them, he wants to rip off his clothes and join in their sensual dance.

"But you are already here with us, you have always been right here with us, you will always be here with us." He hears them call to him.

He needs nothing further, the thought triggers a wild train of imagination, of half understood intuitions of the past that pour forth hinting at the interconnection of all beings, and things. They are an illuminating golden chain strung between the stars revolving wildly in ecstasy. The distinction between the living and the dead disintegrates, washes away, becomes meaningless; the logs are sacred, one with the subterranean strata of existence. He sees that everything comes from the one, is the one and returns to the one power. The vision runs through him until it consumes him. It overpowers him, he no longer sees with his eyes. He is lost in waves of light channeling through the tissue of his mind.

"Holla? What are you doing Gringo?"

Jeff awakens and realises he has gone to sleep on the top of a stack of hay bundles in a barn. A mexican farmer is gesturing to him to come down from the haystack.

"Get out of here crazy Gringo."

Jeff recalls walking in the desert and chasing the three wise men but does not know how he got in the barn. "Funny, I don't remember finding the barn. At least it was warm and the straw was easy to sleep on."

The farmer laughs and mimics Jeff who has acquired a limp from the night's antics. Jeff jumps from the hay and scurries out of the barn happy to leave the startled farmer. He tries to account for his night under the Mexican stars.

A Walk In the Park

Jeff grasps her hand firmly as she guides him across the meadow of an open field in the park. It is late afternoon and it has been raining, not hard, it has been a warm drizzle leaving a cover of wet on the surface of the newly cut grass. Liz is guiding him to her lair, she is anxious to be alone with him.

For a moment there is a rainbow behind her, he sees it for an instant as he puts his hand up to block the sun from his eyes. It is only momentary. It vanishes when he lets his hand drop. He plants his feet firmly, forcing her to stop and watch a group of old men and women lawn bowl. She is frustrated, she is eager to take him home. Desire flames within and guides her actions, lately she has been lusting for him often.

"Let's watch them bowl." He has finally grasped the game and learned some of its rules. To her it is a stupid game and she is annoyed he wants to watch it now, She wants to rip his clothes off and ride him all afternoon. She puts her lust aside and gives in, and takes a seat.

"Oh alright, but you do this all the time. It's boring." In truth, it is the third time this week he has forced her to watch lawn bowling. He finds it fascinating.

"This won't last long, the game is almost over."

He has nowhere to go but home with her. He has no place to hide and he knows it. She knows it too, she will get her way. There is no need for her to be unpleasant. She expects to be pampered, to glitter, to rule. He has learned to live with it. She pulls out a cigarette and holds it up for him to light. When he does, she lets out a long stream of smoke and winks at him, as if to say "good boy."

"I feel I grow closer to the ultimate reality daily." he says this seriously but in a tone that reminds her of someone saying "pass the butter" at the dinner table.

In truth it doesn't matter what he says, she never really listens. Liz licks his ear and whispers agreement. "Yes I believe you are. " Her response is calculated to brush aside conversation. By agreeing to his absurd notion she has closed the subject and there can be no further discussion of it.

She has been trying to create a position of dependence in him, and until recently has been unable to obtain it. She knows that he has run out of places to hide and is coming to accept her dominance now. He is not strong but fate has waited until now to let him fall face first into the net, the trap her dream has nurtured. Knowing that the time is very close when he will have to surrender completely she is deliriously happy. He will soon do her bidding all the time, without resistance.

"The reality of matter is that all things are interrelated...." his voice trails off as he realises no one is listening, especially not her. He wonders about the waves in his voice as they move outward from his larynx. When does the wave stop and become so small it no longer exists?

"Does the coast of China diminish when I drop my spoon from the table?" He asks her. She rubs his butt and pinches the cheeks while fingering the opening of his butt crack.

To her, his madness is delightful, a mark of genius, something to display and parade before the world. It makes her proud. So what if no one understands him? She feels he is inspired and should not be taken lightly. Only she can take him lightly and she picks the spots where she will do it.

"You view things from such a deep level." Her eyes enlarge and her mouth hangs wide to express amazement, her timing is perfect. He smiles shyly at her, flattered. All seems well and the rainbow is back over her shoulder for an instant. He feels her love and adoration.

"You're so easy to please." Liz teases him. Terror, and fear light up his face and she wishes she had never spoken. She has slipped, taken a false step. She wants to let the transgression pass, it is clear he does not like her condescending attitude. He wants equality in their relationship. It is something she will never agree to.

He thinks but does not say:"There must be some other woman out there, someone less deserving, someone with whom I will gain the edge." He can feel it is true and wants to shout it in her face. "I can do better, woman. You need to be careful with what you say."

"The game is very close." he nods towards the lawn bowling changing the subject to avoid further confrontation.

"Yes they seem to be evenly matched teams," she answers.

"It's a matter of luck who will win," he notes.

"Yes," she agrees, happy for the diversion.

A ring of balls surrounds the jack with one throw left to go. They watch as it rolls with deadly precision, winding through the ring and striking the jack, knocking it off the playing field to win the game.

"A matter of luck,"they cry out together, glad to be able to agree on something.

Liz has had enough of his idleness and pulls him away. She wants to go home and make love. The desire is pulling at her, and she lets him know what she wants.

She owns a small flat on the top floor of a high rise, to her it is a palace, and she has been good enough to share it with him. He thinks of it as a dungeon on the tenth floor. The building is the tallest in the south part of town and towers above those around it. The sign on the entrance says "The Towers".

It is late afternoon and the lobby is full of old retired men and women with walkers and canes. There is a low hum of idle chatter as they enter. She is the youngest resident in the building and the subject of much gossip. Some eyes greet their entrance sharply and others look vacantly out to the street pretending not to see them at all.

Her "palace" is on the top floor and has a view of the bay. The desk clerk smiles, they nod back in unison. She pushes the "up" button and summons the elevator. It arrives, they get in together and she pushes the button for the top floor. He lets the door begin to close and then steps out at the last moment.

"Go on alone, I will take the stairs." He separates in rebellion. She is crushed. He sees her cringe and loves it. Triumphant, her despair spurs him on.

"It will be a long climb." She calls out as the door closes.

"Good let her worry, let her wait". He thinks. He has served notice that he is his own man. "Serves her right."

She arrives alone and sighs, "How nice to be looking down at the world below.."

Liz wonders if she should go out in search of him. She is afraid to offend him, that is the problem, of course, she has already offended him. She cannot be sure what she has done, it could be anything, he is so moody. She cultivates her role as patroness, protectress, a role she revels in, a role which she relishes. It gives her the illusion of being in control. He will be along, she is sure of it, so she sits and watches the traffic below.

Jeff stumbles uncertain down the hall looking for the right door. They are all closed and they all look the same, he has forgotten her number, but he knows he will find it.

" In all actions no matter how vague they may seem to be there is always a predetermined reasoning that guides it." He reassures himself. All things are always exactly as they should be.

"It hardly matters if we ourselves recognise it." He knocks on a random door, not sure if it is hers or not.

"Come in," a strange voice interrupts his thoughts. The door has opened for him, he imagines an allure in her eyes but cannot be sure, He does not know her. He has an impression of wrinkles and traces of lines on her face that seem like a road map. He follows her voice faithfully. Her apartment is hot and humid, it is full of tropical plants growing in pots with heat lamps shining on them. They give off a sweet smell. It should be tranquil but he feels a presence, a threat of some kind.

"Relax," she says, "it is only Baby."

"Baby?' he is now certain that his feeling of fear is justified. A motion of a mobile living pipe with patterned colors crawls around her making a spiral that winds up from her legs and rises above her head. A triangle head with its tongue flashing and red eyes glaring jabs at the air and seems to menace him.

"Baby," she answers while stroking the snake's smooth belly, "meet Baby."

Jeff falls frantically against the door that has closed behind him. He is locked in with her, this woman who has invited him to betray his one true love. He feels caged and knows he has made a mistake leaving his protectress waiting. She is just on the floor above, he has been a fool to wander.

"No need to worry, he is friendly, he is a pet." The old woman tries to reassure him and makes her voice sound soothing, and pleasing. Jeff's mind races trying to think of a way out. He lacks the nerve to just exit but he wants to leave. The snake has wound itself around his legs and is starting to squeeze.

The witch rises, sheds her clothes and walks into a sunken bath whose steam fills the air and caresses her skin. She parts her lips and her legs in unison gesturing to him to join her. Baby unwinds and frees him. The snake slithers from sight and hides in the foliage that dominates the room. Gone but not forgotten, Jeff still feels Baby's presence lurking, waiting for him to move if he does the wrong thing.

"You have a snake, as big around as a coffee can, I saw it." he can barely get it out, it seems preposterous. Perhaps he may have imagined it but he is sure he didn't. The woman grins showing missing teeth for the first time, she has taken out a false bridge and makes a circle with her mouth.

She sinks in the water letting her breasts bob and float on the foam. He sees they are large and wrinkled. She moves her hands asking him to come in, rippling the water gently as she does so.

"You're not listening." he complains.

Liz conjures up a look of understanding. No matter how weird he gets, she has access to this look, and can call it forward. She uses it, her look of compassion when she wants to dispel whatever fantasy he is engulfed in. She sees his face now circled by his hands making him seem doll-like, and innocent in the frame he has made.

"Come to bed" she begs him , his body tenses in a reactive response. Their place is very small and constricted. They have one bedroom and it is barely large enough for a double bed. They have a tiny living room with an old couch and frayed filthy rugs.. The television is a black and white and makes use of an antenna in order to get reception. They spend their days watching fuzzy pictures on the few channels available.

He feels like he is in a straight jacket and it is squeezing the life out of him. He becomes aware that there is no snake and no pool of water, he is in the only home he knows with his protectress and she is aging before his eyes. He remembers the lush foliage that was here a moment earlier but it has vanished as if it never existed. In a flash of inspiration he knew there never was a snake.

"Living here is like being in the grasp of a snake." He shouts at her. He wants to run, she has her arms outstretched asking for him to come to her. He is trapped, "There must be something better, some place where I don't have to put up with this bullshit." He knows he has no choice, he cannot be saved.

"Come to bed." Liz repeats herself, annoyed that he has not responded as she had hoped.

"You are a whore. You are the memory of a whore." he spits it out with venom knowing he has cut her deeply.

"Why are you saying that?" She says meekly, looking at his cold, hard, and unforgiving face. He is so cruel, so ruthless, so without compassion, she shudders at his words and feels his loathing. She tries to hide the depth of her hurt, she no longer wants to hear him, she closes her heart and mind to him. She hopes he cannot see her tears, she cannot stop the tears.

"You bitch". He slams the door as he leaves her. A smile breaks on his face. He takes a flight of stairs to the roof. A warm wind blows in from the seas, the city stretches below. He sees a steamer leaving port in the harbor and imagines that he is on it. He breathes easy and tries to forget her crying below. Then it comes to him, "What have I done?" "What have I done? How can I explain it?"

"It was the jungle garden, and the snake, it was their fault." Of course it was, I am innocent and have nothing to do with what happened. "It was that damn snake. I am sure she will forgive me once she understands that it was the snake's fault." But then something in his consciousness reminds him that there was no snake, and no jungle and maybe, just maybe it was his fault.

The Good and The Bad Get Ugly

Liz is sound asleep in the front seat of the car. Her body is exhausted from the effort required to get ready and go out to the movies. The drive-in was her idea but she has passed out totally exhausted.

"I am bored and want to go out." She had demanded that they go to see her hero. She stamped her foot and got her way.

Jeff knew they were disobeying her Doctor's orders which specifically called for two weeks of bed rest. She was told not to strain herself and to lie in bed inactive. But instead she followed her instinct and dragged him to bed and made love with him. Then she decided they had to go out to the movies. It was the latest spaghetti western and she "had" to see it. She dressed as if they were going to a formal occasion and forced him to do as she commanded.

They had arrived at the drive-in and parked close enough to get a fine view of the movie . But now she was fast asleep having ingested a generous quantity of opiates. She had been taking them with abandon ever since she had come home.

They killed the pain if she took enough of them, and masked her stiffness and aches.

This time she overdid it. Her plan was to make sure she controlled the threshold of pain. But she had taken way too many pills and was now fast asleep. Jeff did not like spaghetti westerns. But she got her way and there he was with the speakers hooked up in the window, and the car tilted up towards the screen. It had taken a massive effort for her to stay awake long enough to get dressed. Jeff drove them, even though he did not like driving at night while stoned. It was always a harrowing experience. He had trouble with oncoming lights.

He could not watch the movie, it was strange and almost without dialogue. Liz was comatose and completely oblivious. Jeff gently took the purse from her hands without waking her. He retrieved her bottle and took two of the little white pills. He then put a quantity in his pocket for later use.

"She won't miss them, but if she does, what of it? I'll just deny it."

Anyway, he thought, they shared everything, especially drugs, so why should this be any different? He hoped they were as strong as she had said. He wanted to get really stoned.

As he leaned back against the car door, her face fell and rested with her head lying in his groin. Her breath was hot and came in long heavy heaves. It feels as if she is blowing on his penis. She has aroused him, and is unaware of the effect she is having on him.

The sound coming from the speaker hanging on the car window is getting louder and louder. A three way gun fight is about to start and the combatants are at angles staring each other down. The camera shifts from one face to another and all three are sure they will have to fight the other two. No one wants to go first. It seems inevitable that one or all are about to die. Jeff would rather be on the roof of the hotel smoking a joint and staring out to sea. He is only here at her insistence and she is sleeping through it.

"You have a crush on blue eyes." Jeff accuses her. "Blue eyes" is the star of the movie, and a former television cowboy.

"He's a punk!" Jeff is jealous and angry.

Liz starts snoring with her face buried in his thin pants. Her hot heavy breathing makes the blood throb between his legs. Jeff is becoming erect, his pants have formed a little tent. He is at a crossroads, should he try to wake her? She turns her head upward and he sees her face, peaceful and serene. She smiles sweetly.

"This is so frustrating!," he mutters to himself.

Jeff grabs the hair on the back of her head and rubs his penis in her sleeping face. He savors it completely. She snorts again, louder this time, and seems to wake. It hardly matters to him that she is asleep. She often sucks his dick, but not tonight so far. She is too doped up and sleeping soundly.

"It was a waste of time to bring you here." Jeff is hot and restless. "You're missing the movie."

Her face is sweet and unresponding.

"I've got to go to the bathroom, do you want some popcorn? I know I want some popcorn." Jeff opens the driver's side door and slips out. She slumps face down on the seat of the car filling the space he vacated. She does not stir and remains completely oblivious to his leaving.

"Too much dope." The night air is cold and serves to invigorate his already energized body.

The bathroom and refreshment stand are in the back of the lot where the movie projector is beaming the movie up to the big screen. All the rows are full of cars, he has to pick his way through the entanglement of speaker wires connecting the cars to the utility poles. It is a confusing maze.

Jeff is unsteady and stumbles in the darkness, the gravel in the lot is slippery. He loses his balance and starts to fall. He grabs a speaker wire and yanks on it trying to stay upright. The speaker comes out of its holder and smashes against the car window.

"Shit" he steadies himself on the hood of a stranger's car. He has made a crack in the window. He rights himself.

"Hey what the fuck? Watch out!", a high pitched female voice chastises him.

It is a woman alone and she slides across the seat to
see the damage he has done. She is smoking. She tries to put
out her cigarette but the ashtray is full. Her burning butt
falls on the floor. It begins to burn a whole in her carpet.

"Fuck" she dives down to retrieve the butt.

"Hey man what's the matter with you?" She rolls down the
window and sticks her head out trying to see the large crack
he has made. Marijuana smoke billows out from her car. She
has unrolled the window and her speaker crashes to the
ground.

"God Dammit man, you must be fucked up, you cracked
my window." She shoves her head out of the window, and
squints at him. "Far out!"

"What's far out?" he asks.

She grabs him by the neck and yanks him into the car. "I like
your beard man. Far out!"

She attempts to pull him through the window. Jeff sees that
her pants are down and her panties are down as well. What
has she been doing?

"Sorry about the window, it was an accident." She is on her knees pulling Jeff's head until he can see her naked crotch.

"Don't worry about the damn window, it's not my car. Get in here. The beard makes you look like the devil. I always wanted to fuck the devil." She is rough and older. Thirty or more, She has long straight dark hair.

"Stop pulling, I'm tangled up." His penis is hard again and now it has a place to go. The universe is providing, he smiles.

People in the adjoining cars are annoyed. They are shouting at him. He opens her door and plunges forward. She rocked backward and freed her legs from her pants and panties and put her legs up in the air inviting him. She pulls his face into her pussy wrapping her legs around his head. She squeezes hard..

"Love your beard!" She moans as he wraps his mouth and tongue around her clitoris. He sucks on it moving it back and forth between his teeth. He rubs it with his beard. "I always wanted to fuck the devil. Are you the devil?"

Her hand grabs his penis and squeezes it hard. She moves it up and down in a piston motion. Jeff is stiff and growing harder. She guides him to her hole. She is crazy wet and wraps her hand around his buttocks and pulls him in with as much force as she can muster.

"Am I your first Indian girl?" her eyes twinkle as she asks him.

Jeff feels a bit dizzy. He has trouble making out her words. She is talking but he does not understand a word. He is plunging into her as deeply as he can. He is moving slower and slower allowing each thrust to reach its deepest penetration point. His brain has slowed down. Instead of the violent rocking he expects, it has become like a slow waltz. The shock absorbers of the car are making noises in unison with their mutual motions. He becomes aware that she is making a lot of noise. Are they attracting too much attention? How could he explain this?

"What?" he manages to speak between the friction and the screaming.

"I am Indian, am I your first?"

"Nah, I'm not a virgin. You nuts?" He doesn't want to talk.

"I'm Sioux?" she mutters. She can feel he is getting ready to shoot out his load.

"Sue?" his body jerks and he shoots out a stream of liquid. It jerks again and again as he spasmodically completes the deed.

"I'm married, you know." She has orgasmed many times.

"Married?" Jeff asks, startled. He wonders where her man is? Is he about to open the door and find me? He starts to panic. "Are you nuts?"

"My husband is in jail for selling cocaine. He got caught in this drive-in a year ago selling to a narc."

"Crap you're weird." He is angry and wants to leave.

"Quiet you'll wake my son."

"Are you kidding?" She had been carrying on like a banshee for the last twenty minutes, and now she asks for quiet?

Jeff realises a toddler standing in a diaper is peering at him from the back seat. Jeff puts on underpants and searches for his pants.

"Christ, why didn't you say something?" He wonders, has the kid watched the whole thing?

"It's alright, it's just Sonny. Say hello Sonny." Jeff realises that she is thin, almost skeletal. He can see her ribs and her little breasts and tiny nipples in the moonlight. Sonny opens his arms wide and squeals with glee.

"He needs a father, he has forgotten his real father." Her voice cracks as she speaks.

A wave of uneasiness rushes over Jeff, he has been used, caught in a trap. What if she didn't use any protection? What if she has a disease?

Urges beyond his control had been at work, he had been used by a power greater than himself for a purpose he did not understand. It made him shudder.

"You alone?" The woman was sobering up..

"No." He nods towards the front of the lot hoping to avoid any discussion.

"As soon as I saw you I knew you were the one." Her voice is full of hope.

She realises she is looking for something or someone.

"When I was thirteen, I left my body during the chanting, the drumming. I hovered above it and felt free. I saw myself moving in the line, I hung above myself and tonight it happened again. I saw you coming in the lot, searching for me."

Sonny squeals and laughs trying to throw his arms around Jeff's neck. What if I have made her pregnant? The thought frightens him, he does not want to think about it. He has visions of an outcast child wandering alone in the world and it is his fault. Suddenly his mind has leapt ahead, how could it be otherwise? Of course, this is a curse, she has brought a curse down upon me. The child will grow to be a man and one day he will find me.

Jeff panics,he tries to pry Sonny off his neck. Sonny has a wad of spit rush up and it splays out on Jeff's neck and drips onto his shirt.

"A madman will shoot me like a dog on the street, and only I will know it is my son." Jeff looks at her with rage in his eyes. "All because of you."

"Are you a crazy man?" His eyes are flashing and he looks like he is possessed. "Get out of here man." She pushes him away hard.

"He'll find me like a magnet. He'll think he is crazy and yet he will know and he will kill me because of what we have done here." Jeff has worked himself into a frenzy.

"Get out of here, you're nuts." She has crawled up in the corner of the car and is trying to hide behind the steering wheel. Sonny starts to cry and screech. He knows something is wrong and fears for his mother. Jeff backs out of the car with his eyes glued on her.

"You're the devil man, I know you are." She spits it at him with a snake like venom.

Jeff flees, leaving the two. "Popcorn" he remembers I am after Popcorn. He finds his way to the stand and buys a bag.

As Jeff approaches the car he sees she is still sleeping peacefully. He opens the door and she wakes with a sweet smile and a look of contentment.

"Do you want some popcorn?" He holds the bag out toward her.

Liz shakes her head yes and takes some. " I had a beautiful dream about us."

He slides in beside her and gives her a kiss. "Tell me about it." He puts his arm around her. The movie is almost over, it is time to go home.

The Ancient Summons and the Mountain Shack

From where Jeff is standing, the entire valley has unfolded. It has been lit by the last glance of gold cast by the sun as it sets in the west. A fire crackles, and the smell of beans and broth boiling on a hearth, please his nostrils. He is hungry and alert, his blood races. Jeff feels he is being watched, because he is always being watched. Out of the corner of his eye he sees someone leaning on the cabin doorway. Jeff turns and acknowledges the stranger who is leering at him with a toothy grin.

"Come in and eat," he calls Jeff.

There is a buzz in the air, a hum, it is complementing the stillness of the approaching night. It is gnats hovering over a dirty little pool of stagnant water, the last remnants of a dried up stream. He listens more closely, it is not gnats, no, it is a chant, a chant issuing from the hollow of a giant redwood across the meadow.

It becomes clear that Mike and Ed are harmonizing, it is their voices he hears. Their chant announces their absorption, they are one, life is one. For a brief moment, they have become a resilient pool, vibrating and reflecting everything the sunlight casts into them. It is twilight and the sunlight is getting weak, soon they will be reflecting moonlight. In a flash he realises that they are mirroring whatever the world has to offer. They are at peace. He wants to join them. To celebrate with them.

Insects cover his face. They invade his nostrils, they fill his lungs. He chokes and coughs trying to breathe. The buzz moves into his ears, they are beating against his ear drum. He feels an uncomfortable tickle as they force their way into his inner ear. He slaps and rubs his head violently trying to remove them. They persist.

"I'm coming," he calls to the man who has stepped from the porch and disappeared back into the cabin. Jeff follows him, desperate to escape the nasty swarm.

"You have never been here before," The tranquil voice greets him.

"I was invited for the weekend. It is my first time. Mike has come before." Jeff affirms what they both know, he has never been here before.

"No one stays the weekend here."

"But I was invited to stay the weekend." Jeff is disturbed by the force of conviction in the man's voice.

"No doubt, still it will not be easy for you to stay for only two days. You may manage it. Not likely though." There is no threat in his voice, only a calm certainty. "Have a piece of bread. It is homemade."

Jeff takes the bread and chews it unconsciously. The cabin is one large open room with a long loft overhead. Mattresses hang over the edge of the loft. There is a small open kitchen with a tiny table and two chairs. In the far back hand corner is a bathroom sink, with a toilet sitting out in the open air. The toilet is broken, a fact made obvious by the non stop sound of running water. There are trays of food, mostly sweets, lying on the kitchen table. Jeff finishes the bread and meanders over and picks up a brownie.

"You are fortunate, Ed only allows a fortunate few to stay here and receive the communion. He has judged you as worthy.

"Communion?" Jeff is suspicious of the word.

"It will find you on its own, if you stay here long enough." The man was talking in riddles.

"Find me? Who will find me?"

"Hand me a brownie, and have another yourself."

Jeff realises that he has already eaten the first brownie. He decides another would be nice. As he hands the stranger one he begins to feel heavy. He is feverish, and flushed and sits down to rest. He finds himself collapsing into a bean bag chair. Something has reached out and pulled him to the ground. He is pinned in the chair. The bag molds around his body. The running water in the background has become musical, it is almost symphonic in nature. A soft percussion-like sound joins in. What could that be? He wonders if it is the sound of his own heart.

The song is joined by a quick rhythmical tapping noise. It is the sound of water dripping from the faucet, but it has been magnified a hundred times. Combining with the drums. The drips provide a full and resonant chorus. He cannot lift his hand. It is as if a door has opened and he has been swallowed, pulled violently into the center of the Earth.

Jeff's first urge is to fight against it, but there is nothing there to fight. His inner voice says,"The harder you push, the tighter the coil's grasp will become." He relaxes, they ease up,

"They have come for you." It is the stranger's voice. It is distant and faint. Jeff can see that the stranger has not moved. He is sitting in exactly the same spot, just across the room. Jeff wonders why he sounds so far away.

He struggles and tries once more to break free from the tight grip that is holding him motionless. He begins to float, there is the sound of rushing air. A powerful energy, one originating in the pit of his stomach, has risen up through his spine and into his skull. He feels like he is riding the wind. Somehow he knows it is not wind or air he is caught in, instead it is energy and consciousness. The words, "I have been emancipated" echo in his brain. Even as this happens, he knows his body is still pinned in the chair. His mind hovers over his body, as it sits lifeless in the chair unable to move.

He watches with amusement. He sees that he is dazed, but his "watching mind" is sharp and clear. Is this freedom I am feeling? Am I free? What am I?

The Stranger passes his hand before Jeff's eyes trying to wake him. He laughs, and continues passing his hands back and forth in front of Jeff's stone cold face. He seems to be finding Jeff's frozen state amusing. His facial muscles twitch, he is laughing, always laughing! The laughter comes in waves that leave sparkling trails of light in the air.

Jeff has slipped in between the visual reality of lips moving and the sound waves they are generating! It occurs to him that he has speeded up and his mind is moving faster than the events he is witnessing. He tries to hold the thought in place. It is like throwing an anchor over the side of a speeding ship.

He cannot move, not a muscle, and knows there must be a reason he feels so paralyzed.

"After a while you will be able to move again." It is the stranger's voice.

No sound accompanies the message which is ringing clearly in his mind. It is strung on a telepathic wire and has reached straight to the core of his being. It is his choice. He could reject contact but he receives it. But what is the message? Should he listen? He is not sure.

"No arrival here is accidental, none come by chance."

Jeff wishes to ask a question and intuitively realises that he already has done so. Will he be answered? His filtering mechanisms are auditing everything that enters and leaves his mind. It is a protection, a barrier, stopping mental overload.

"No one could live if all the possibilities inherent in their minds were developed and laid open to their access and use."

The voice makes clear what he sensed. He sees that the mechanism is protecting him and always has. It is a part of his own mind. He is relieved.

"You are warned not to tamper." The voice is calm and firm.

"Yes you are that ignorant." the voice anticipates his doubts.

"The planes exist and you can enter, but if you force entry, the risk is great." The voice speaks with a melodic solemnity.

"Artificial entry is forbidden." The voice burns a fire in Jeff's brain.

The word "forbidden" becomes a fire burning in his mind's eye, the fire becomes a hot white light, and at the base of the light Jeff imagines he sees a pair of calm steady eyes gazing at him. What is this center where I am? Jeff is aware of the voice, as only voice and not light, not eyes, only voice without sound.

"Remember, entry using artificial means is forbidden."

A hand crosses Jeff's field of vision, it is blocking the ceiling light as it passes. The hand stops and rests on Jeff's forehead.

"What happened?" The Stranger's voice is very worried.

"You don't know?" Jeff wakes to see his concern is genuine.

"You were walking across the room and then you just fell. You fell into the chair. You passed out."

The Stranger puts his hand on Jeff's head again.

"You're burning up. Are you alright?"

"Yes, I think so." Jeff wonders who is behind the "Eyes" that spoke? "Yes, I am fine."

The Reactor-- Elective Affinities

Jeff cracks the car window letting the smoke rush
out. He sees the reactors, nestled in between, two hills
below. From a distance, they each look like half an egg shell
fastened to the ground. They are secured by a belt of
concrete ringing a circle around them.

She has taken him down this road before, telling and
retelling her stories about accidents that might have
occurred. Stories about near meltdowns, and how they had
been accompanied with accusations of cover up. Regardless
of what happened in the past there are two reactors below
and they are still operational. It wasn't something that he
cared about. If she cared, it was her business to worry, not
his.

"That's where I'm taking you." She nodded towards the
concrete bulbs. "They offer a tour."

"That's the big surprise? I got up early for this?" She had
really built this trip up, and he was anticipating something
spectacular. This fell short and he was disappointed in her.
She had a penchant for creating mystery and she expected
indulgence. He indulged her always, it was part of the price
he paid to be with her.

"How interesting," he said, hoping to actually sound interested.

She turned down a narrow service road and followed a sign marked "Visitors Parking". Theirs was the only car in the lot. She pointed to an arrow saying "Visitors This Way" directing them towards the first dome.

"You see people do come here. That's why they need the sign."

She was using her "cheerful" voice. He didn't answer, instead he grimaced and turned his face away. She led him to the entrance.

Inside were displays explaining the history of atomic energy and the process used to make it available safely to the public. Jeff's eyes rolled up in his head as she read out loud one of the plaque's. He wondered if she thought he couldn't read.

An immense pressure throbbed in his skull and a violent light flashed before his eyes momentarily blinding him. It was as if she had an electric drill in her hands and was painstakingly drilling into the top of his skull. A red film coated the back of his eyelids and air bubbles floated in the liquid at the corner of his eyes. He felt the ground move with tremors causing him to lurch forward swaying dizzily into her.

"I am..it's coming back..I'm on the edge of seeing it...." he mumbles.. She strains to hear him but can not understand a word.

In his mind's eye he is wearing a long flowing robe that trails from his shoulders to the ground. It is a magnificent garb and has appeared magically in place of the shorts and t-shirt he had slipped that morning.

Everything becomes clear to him in an instant. They are in charge! They have been transported to a hidden inner chamber. A control room above an altar where a blue fire is burning. Below a chanting priest is making offerings.

"I control the apparatus, not the priest." he speaks to her with fervor. She wipes his brow with a handkerchief. They are the only ones in the exhibit, she looks to see if there are cameras recording the scene.

She locates the camera and smiles at it! Her smile says there is no reason for panic, nothing is out of the ordinary here. She knows it has started once again. She smiles for the camera. We do not require assistance, she combats the faintness she feels, What is he going to do next?

"The priest relies on me, on us." He assures her she has a role to play. She listens and does not answer.

"The power level is rising, but it needs to go higher." He says with authority!

Jeff is in tune with his inner priest, it's all about obedience. The multitude is expecting and calling for a miracle, for a display of the divine.

"The power is in my hands, I control it." Jeff yells at the Priest who does not react.

Bolts of lightning fly across the room and clash, making sparks of electricity explode and cascade in all directions. There is a glazed distant look in the Priest's eyes. He slashes the air making trails that leave tracing in the glorious light show hc has created.

"I stand above it, I control it." Jeff continues to yell at the Priest who is ignoring him.

She looks at the cameras worried. She comes to him to stop his frenzy. He feels her touch, warm and urgent against his cheek, she centers him. For a moment he sees that they are standing alone in the display room of the power plant. There is no Priest, no lightning. He smiles gently at her, grateful for her presence. Where am I? Where are we?

She joins him. They are on the edge of something important. For weeks she has been having the same dream over and over again, and somehow it involved this place. This exhibit where her father had brought her to explain his work.

"You fool, do not reveal the Inner Secrets!" Jeff yells at the Priest who has adjusted the power volumes.

The dull glass cabinets explain what was once so important to her father. They hold the answer to the mystery that she knows is alive between Jeff and herself. She sees in his reaction to it all that she is right, but she needs to hear it from him. To find out what it is all about. Who is the inner Priest? Where does he come from? She must find out.

"I wasn't wrong to bring you here but I was afraid to tell you why." She wants him to understand her past.

"You ignorant fool, you are tampering and dealing in mysteries you can never understand!" Jeff tries again to capture the attention of the Priest.

She has been looking for Jeff to take the lead. She had hoped he knew the answer to the riddle and could tell her. Instead he only stares blankly at her. He is still too far away. She shakes him hard.

He has found her out. He knows who she really is now. She can no longer hide. She runs the control room with him. She has accepted her role. The once dull grey sweater she was wearing has become an elegant purple robe, just like his, marking her as a priestess of the highest order.

Together they are tapping a mysterious and powerful energy. They are sending massive bolts of power winging through the sky, and moving great stone blocks that hide the hidden chambers of the sacred heart from the profane. Layer by layer, they are building a cosmic sundial that will chart the destiny of all to come for centuries. He sees the puppet priest below, around him the crowd of worshipers are silently waiting. Jeff looks into her eyes, "It is no dream."

"Of course not," she answers back. But for her it has all been about the dreams. What does he see? The room is quiet and they are all alone. She imagines her father silently looking out from behind a closed door and sobs a little to herself. She is afraid Jeff may be insane and she may be crossing the line and joining him in his madness.

"I didn't know precisely what would happen," she tries to explain. "I had to bring you here."

She knows she has had a part in everything that has happened. In her dream something took flight between them in this room. She had hoped for a new beginning, but the real content of the dream always slipped from her long before she could get it to completely take form. It was illusive and seductive.

"We alone know, we alone are trusted. We hold the key." He is grateful for her help. The work is sacred. When she is wearing the robe she is his trusted partner.

She sees he is fixated on something she cannot see, he is moving his hands in the air, motioning! It seems that he is doing something, but there is nothing there to do. He is playing with dials and levers, but she sees nothing but empty air. Uncertain on how to play the game, she slips behind him and whispers in his ear,

"What should I do?"

He flashes a glare of anger and annoyance, this is a critical point in the coming ceremony, they must be ready to release the divine essence, the timing between them be flawless, and she is asking what to do?

"Do not betray my trust. It is almost time." His warning is ominous.

The worshippers are in a frenzy. Ready to merge into the one true being. It is time. Jeff forces the psychic engines of the machine into full throttle, it glows with a tremendous throbbing white heat. Their minds and souls are combined into one being, as energy from the core crackles and lights the sky. The crowd is exhausted and lies prone in front of the sun Priest. Jeff nods at her with a look of satisfaction, all is well. He raises his hands to the sky in joy.

Of course, in her mind she has been stomping her foot on the ground in a meaningless way, and she knows it. She panics, she does not belong and it has all gone wrong.

"Have I done it right?" she cries out desperate to be reassured. She has been moving aimlessly and thinks that she has failed. If she fails him, what will he do?

He rushes to help her. She has been almost perfect; he cannot let her fail, they must remain hidden in their role of master priests. No one can see behind the illusion. The worshipers cannot become aware of their presence.

"Just in time." He says suddenly with a sigh of relief. She nods in agreement.

"Do you understand what was done?" he asks.

"No" she wants to tell him about the recurring dreams that had forced her to bring them here but she cannot do it. She listens and waits. What does he think? " I was trying to find a way to reach you. To connect with you."

"Can I help you?" An attendant has appeared and seems anxious about them. She wonders what the attendant has seen, have they been betrayed? Has he found them out?

"We were just leaving. Do not worry about us please." She pulls Jeff towards the exit. He looks sheepishly at her, why is she so upset? Why are we leaving? We have only just arrived. He lets her take the lead and follows her to the car.

"Why did you bring me here?" he asks her.

"I don't know, I was hoping you would know the answer to that question." she says disappointed.

Where the Snows of Yesteryear Have Gone

Although the apartment is empty Jeff feels a presence. It is a feeling that is often with him. No motion, no thought, no particle of existence is unimportant. Each thing belongs in its time and place exactly as it is and nothing can be otherwise. In addition to holding a belief in the exact precision and unity of all things, he is certain all life is all being monitored in some way. He is certain that the monitoring is being done by a personality. He ponders this idea but soon understands it is too vague to be an idea, instead it is more of a feeling. An eerie feeling of being watched all the time.

He reaches for a deck of cards, shuffles them and lays them out to play solitaire. The first card he turns up is the Jack of Spades. He hears the front door open and turns to see her enter in her beach clothes. She has been up on the roof sunbathing and reading. It makes him suspicious, her leaving him and going alone to the roof. Who was up there? Did she meet someone?

"Anyone up there?" he asks her. He keeps turning cards, he is winning, they are matching up well.

"Naw, I was the only one." She shuffles into the bedroom dropping her towel and book on the ground and flops onto the bed. She falls so hard that the bed springs jangle with the impact of her body. She lets out a loud hissing cry by blowing air between her teeth.

The racket she makes grinds on him, she breaks his chain of thought, the delicate structure his imagination has been building crumbles in her carelessness.

"If I knew how we got here, I mean if I could control my own past, I could set us straight," He wonders if she is listening. She does not answer or acknowledge what he said. "I feel trapped, one step out of the moment. Why are you doing this to me?" He asks, baffling her.

He waits for an answer but she says nothing. Jeff turns up as the final Ace, it assures him of winning the game. Damn it, why is she silent? She does not appreciate him, the way she entered the room made that clear.

"You have no sense of inner space." he says in a near whisper. He is unsure if she heard him, then he hears the sound of regular deep breathing and knows she has fallen asleep.

"She has no sense of the nature of the higher realities," he continues his monologue. He hears sheets rustle as she rolls in her sleep and turns her head away from him.

He wins the game of solitaire and decides to play again. He gathers the cards into a deck and evens the edges by banging them loudly on the coffee table. He glances at her to see if the sudden noise has had any effect on her sleep. He imagines that she has wrinkled her nose a little bit in annoyance. He pounds the cards again, this time a little harder. He imagines that she has turned towards him with a grimace on her face. If only he could enlighten her, make her aware of the intense inner life he lives, but he is resigned to the knowledge that the effort will be futile. So far it has always been futile. Why should anything change?

"You are just too dense, enmeshed in daily life." He accuses her. "Too common."

He holds it against her, this lack of awareness on her part. She is small in mind and spirit, even a bit petty at times. He does not want to admit it to himself, but he thinks she is not worthy of him. She will never understand the timelessness he feels, will never be able to see the breadth of the macrocosmic world that stretches out before his inner eye. She will never understand how well centered he is, she will never be able to join him or participate in the spiritual freedom he has found.

"You are earth bound, locked in the material world."

She is sleeping soundly and has not heard a word of his monologue. He gets up and walks to the edge of the bed, careful not to wake her. Her body has made a heavy imprint in the bed. Her long black hair flows casually down her back. She stretches out, curvy in the string bathing suit that reveals her full perfect breasts and ample hips. The absolute peaceful calm in her face irritates him. He grabs her by the ankle and tightens his grip, shaking her well formed leg.

She stirs and smiles up at him happy that he is interested and has his hand so firmly grasping her skin. The tight grip makes him seem masculine, she likes it. She spreads her legs and quivers hoping that her nearly naked body will evoke a reaction in him.

His blood surges and rushes, his heart beats faster and faster. The objects in the room are becoming hazy and distant. The sex urge buffets him, swirling up inside his brain. He is being carried along in a pulsating tide so swift and strong that he begins to feel lost in it. He knows she is sitting now and reaching out to him, but she seems far away and inconsequential.

The orange barrel has taken effect. Time has ground to a halt and he feels that he is suspended, hanging on the outer edges of it.

Perhaps his life is one meaningless action, after another, strung together and somehow tied into a knot. The knot has personality, his personality, he wants to lift himself out of the physical world that has become a tightly bound knot. He wants to untie the knot and flow free in the hot warm surge that he knows is engulfing him. He wants to let go and drown in the energy that has claimed him. He is flowing, flowing with warmth, flowing towards an ocean of love.

She is slapping his face, shaking him, yelling in his ear, but he is far, far away. For a brief second he tries to reach out to her but cannot feel his own body move. Jeff has a fleeting feeling of a great separation, of a tremendous distance between them, but it is useless, it is all an illusion, she is an illusion. He becomes aware that there is only one reality, one force and it is a unity. Nothing has form, she has no form and the vision of her slips away.

He rises and picks up a book she has left by the bedside. It is a novel she has been reading. The cover features a partly dressed woman and in bold letters it has the word **ESCAPE** printed on the cover. He turns it over and over again in his hands. He flashes it at her and grins.

In one last intuitive moment he sees all the compartmented segments of his being become one thing and he knows he is about to be released. He has been granted a great gift; his mind rejoices with a flood of joy. He has been triumphantly blessed with an awakening. He is transmuting and becoming energy.

He heads for the open window smiling and flashing the book cover with the word **ESCAPE** at her over and over again. Intuitively she knows he is going to jump. She races to grab him, to stop him. He slips through her fingers. She screams and watches as he falls ten floors to the ground below. His body hits and bounces a little and she sees pieces of his arms and legs shatter and break as he crashes into the hard cement below. His body is lifeless. Blood is pooling around him. She calls 911 and cries. She gathers up his drugs and hides them. It is best that no one knows the truth. She wonders if anyone ever really knows the truth. She knows the truth is he is gone.

Made in the USA
Coppell, TX
10 June 2021

57212629R00138